From: Delphi@oracle.org

To: C_Evans@athena.edu

Re: U.S. Coast Guard Lieutenant, Nikki Bustillo

Christine,

We've gained information from the former senator. It seems he employed a hacker, known only as Diviner, to track down information about Arachne's whereabouts. Diviner is our next lead.

We've tracked his signal to the Port of Miami, and Nikki Bustillo can help us there. I'll have her use her contacts to find his location. I have a feeling he'll be heading into international waters—with Arachne close behind.

I've got a few assistants in Asia who may be able to aid Nikki. She's not worked with Oracle before, so see if you can send some Athena alum agents her way, for reassurance. She's not one to trust easily.

D.

Dear Reader,

Like Nikki, I often wonder what it would be like to have sisters to have fun with, to cry with and to call upon for help. And also like Nikki, sisters of choice have appeared during times I've needed them, sometimes in the form of renewed relationships with long-distance cousins (Divas rule!) or new relationships with like-minded women whose company and intimacy add greatly to my life on a daily basis.

What intrigued me most while writing this story was how a woman like Nikki—strong and competent – would handle being a fish out of water in Hong Kong, a city and culture both familiar and utterly foreign to her young American mind. I wasn't surprised to discover that in her times of need, it was her relationships with special women that brought her through.

That's what makes the Athena Force series special for me. These books are about independent women who understand their greatest strength lies not just in their own courage, but also in the combined determination of a very unique sisterhood.

All the best,

Sandra

Sandra K. Moore

WITHOUT A TRACE

Silhouette®

ATHENA FORCE

Published by Silhouette Books
America's Publisher of Contemporary Romance

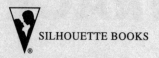

SILHOUETTE BOOKS

ISBN-13: 978-0-373-38979-7
ISBN-10:   0-373-38979-5

WITHOUT A TRACE

Visit Athena Force at www.eHarlequin.com

Printed in U.S.A.

SANDRA K. MOORE

has been a technical writer, poet, martial arts student and software product manager, occasionally all at the same time. She lives on the Texas coast with her handsome partner and a moody tabby cat, and she hopes one day to ride a Ducati sport bike from Hong Kong to Stanley Village. Visit her on the Web at www.sandrakmoore.com.

To all sisters—by blood and by choice—
in a challenging world.

Acknowledgements

This book could never have existed without the help
so generously given by many people:

My thanks and my admiration go out to
Petty Officer 3rd Class Sondra-Kay Kneen, who
serves her country in the U.S. Coast Guard and has
climbed through a bilge or two in her time.

Thanks to Elena Torres-Jovel,
for her help with the Spanish.

I'm especially grateful for my patient editor,
Stacy Boyd, who never fails to see what I'm trying—
and failing—to get on the page, and who is so
gracious when pointing me in the right direction.

And many thanks to Sharron McClellan,
who gave Nikki such a wonderful
big-sister-of-choice in Jess Whitaker.

Chapter 1

Lieutenant Nikki Bustillo knew the shrimp boat her Coast Guard crew had just boarded for inspection was hiding something. It was as plain, she thought wryly, as the nose on her face.

She peered through the boat's rear pilothouse door at the ragged Hispanic crew members lined up in the vessel's stern. Yep. Definitely something wrong. Beneath the stench of day-old shrimp lay the almost overwhelming musk of fear. It emanated from the deckhands as strongly as the diesel fumes off the hot engines. This wasn't about having a net with its turtle extraction devices sewn shut, which was an illegal technique that caught more fish but threatened endangered sea turtles.

No, these crewmen were scared to death.

"Problem?" Ensign Rich Mansfield, the boarding team's rookie member, joined her in the trawler's pilothouse.

"The *Montoya* is carrying more than dinner."

Mansfield gave her a measured look. "How do you know?"

Nikki nodded at the fidgeting shrimper crew. "They look nervous to you?"

"Yeah. Sort of."

The truth was, these men didn't look any more nervous than any other crew Nikki's command had stopped in the past three weeks along Florida's coastline. But to put it mildly, they reeked of fear. Literally. The vessel was definitely carrying something besides shrimp. Cocaine was a good guess.

Mansfield hovered at her elbow as she thumbed through the vessel's shoddily kept logs. She would've had the fresh-out-of-cadet-training ensign pegged merely as a nuisance, except back in February she'd received an encrypted e-mail message from someone called Delphi warning her to watch her back: somebody called Arachne was getting her jollies kidnapping Athena Academy students and alumnae, and Nikki's name was on the wish list.

This Delphi had never contacted her before, but had known too many students—too many facts about too many of Nikki's friends—for Nikki to doubt she knew what she was talking about. Behind that e-mail had come a visit from a former classmate,

Dana Velasco, confirming Delphi's assertion. Nikki had gotten the impression she—Nikki could only think of Delphi as "she"—was never wrong.

And Mansfield had a habit of pestering Nikki with a lot of questions she preferred not to answer.

He'd been particularly intrigued by her schooling. The Athena Academy for the Advancement of Women was unusual and he'd wanted to hear all about it. Fair enough. She'd given him the Cliff's Notes version and moved on to her rapid-fire years at Florida State University studying literature, then to her decision to join the Coast Guard.

The truth was, the Athena Academy was the first place where she'd felt like she belonged. After an early childhood filled with seven raucous older brothers, she'd felt like an all-girls school was somehow coming home. Her orientation group, the Hecates, had consisted of four other girls, each unique, each talented and gutsy and strong. How could she possibly explain her sense of sistership with these women? Especially to someone she didn't know. It didn't seem…right…to share that with a stranger.

After graduation, she'd hoped to put her unique strengths to good use: her eidetic memory, her particularly fine eye-hand coordination and her martial arts skills. Those strengths and a late-blooming love of the sea had led her inevitably to the Coast Guard, where she'd screamed up the command ladder, making lieutenant at twenty-three.

Her ability to unerringly locate the bags of cocaine, heroin bricks and pot stashes? Well, that was just a little something extra given to her when her mom's IVF doctor took a few liberties with her genetic material. It was why she could smell trouble in a man's sweat, and why she'd chosen drug interdiction as her Coast Guard career of choice.

When Delphi told her back in February that she'd been targeted for kidnapping because of her special ability, Nikki had had to take a few days to get adjusted to that reality. Her parents, who'd simply wanted a daughter instead of an eighth son, had applied to the Zuni, New Mexico, fertility lab in an attempt to have one. As far as Nikki knew, the only special order her parents had placed was for gender. And nothing else.

But with the warning from Delphi concerning Athena students with "abilities," Nikki had set about methodically reviewing the files of her fellow crew members, just to cover her bases. Then Mansfield had arrived a month ago and started hanging around her like a bad high school crush.

She regarded him now as he shuffled through greasy work orders and pay slips in a console drawer. Maybe he was just an Anglo with a fascination for Cuban women. Okay, so she was second-generation Cuban-American, born and bred in Arizona, but she knew her way around Spanish—vocabulary was a helluva lot simpler when you had a photographic memory—even if her pronunciation left a little something to be desired.

With Mansfield still at her elbow, she radioed her

captain aboard the cutter *Undaunted* and let him know what was going down.

"Another hunch?" Captain Pickens's voice growled in response.

"Yes, sir."

"Go with it."

"Yes, sir." She turned to Mansfield. "Let's see what they've got in the hold."

She set two members of her boarding team to stand guard over the trawler's captain and crew while the rest fanned out and started a search for drugs.

It had begun as a more or less routine stop. The ancient trawler, common to this part of the south Florida coastline, had looked a bit light as the *Undaunted* cruised into visual range. Normally the bottom paint of a fully loaded shrimp boat lay underwater. This trawler's bottom paint showed a clear six inches out of the water, suggesting that the concrete ballast used to steady the trawler in rough seas had been replaced with something much lighter. Like cocaine.

When Mansfield yanked open the main hatch, fear musk—a cross between burnt coffee and battery acid—surged from the general vicinity of the shrimper captain.

"Got a problem?" Nikki asked the captain in Spanish.

He shrugged, looking sullen, though his gaze kept darting at the guardsmen disappearing into the hold.

"How long have you been piloting this vessel?" Nikki asked the usual questions while her squad members poked through the compartments where the shrimp were stored. The captain muttered his answers, which she jotted down in a small notebook. The *Montoya* rolled gently as fat waves slid beneath her, and the sun glared off the water and steel.

After a few minutes, Mansfield was back, wiping sweat from his face and looking queasy.

"Nothing," he said.

"You've been thorough." She made it a statement, so he'd understand thoroughness was expected, no matter how bad the job stank.

"Yes, ma'am."

Nikki narrowed her eyes at the shrimp boat captain. Burnt coffee assaulted her nostrils. The man was scared, and the strength of the scent couldn't be just because he had more than his allowed catch aboard.

"Look again," she told Mansfield.

"But—" He caught himself before protesting a direct order.

She leveled a measuring gaze at him. Maybe that was why she didn't trust him. Because he couldn't stomach the job. Hell, she knew what that was like, but it didn't mean she'd cut him any more slack than her CO had ever cut her. "You'll get used to it. Come on."

Nikki gripped the edges of the storage hatch, took a deep breath, held it and leaned into the hold. Something hard touched her shoulder; Ensign Artie Jackson held out a heavy-duty flashlight, which she took. Light splashed over the dead shrimp and rusting steel hull. The plastic liner that held the shrimp was cracked and stained from years of use. Stifling heat pressed in on her, bringing a quick burst of sweat to her face and neck. From the looks of it, this shrimp wasn't a fresh catch.

She let go the breath she was holding and sniffed.

The musk of coffee bored past the acrid, salty smell of dead sea creatures and washed over her in a hot wave. Nikki grit her teeth against nausea. Terror. Terror like nothing she'd ever smelled before. Terror and…grief?

She leaned away from the hatch and squinted into the afternoon sun. "Get me a rake or shovel or something!" The wind lifting over the trawler's rail cooled her face.

Jackson handed her a shrimp rake. Nikki coughed hard a few times, then shook herself mentally. *Get a grip. It's just rotting critters.*

The days-old dead sea life she could handle. It was what lay beneath that had her reeling.

She reached the rake down and scraped a bare spot inside the storage unit, then dropped through the deck hatch. A few minutes of hard work had cleared a broad swath, revealing another hinged hatch immediately beneath her feet. It was roughly two feet by two feet, with a pull handle. She would have smiled at her success, but the bitter scent of fear ratcheted her nerves another notch tighter.

Nikki stepped aside, pulled her sidearm, grabbed the handle and yanked the hatch open.

It was like looking into a mass grave. People in

ragged, stained clothing lay piled on each other, huddled, clutching pillowcases or battered backpacks. One, a boy no more than thirteen, stirred and opened his eyes, squinting against the flashlight's beam but too weak to hold up a hand for shade. The rest were still.

"Shit." Nikki raised her head. "We've got refugees! Jackson! Take the captain and crew into custody. Mansfield, radio the captain. We'll need a chopper."

Nikki leaned in and grasped the boy's hand. "I'm here to get you out," she said in Spanish.

The boy struggled to keep his eyes open. "America?"

"Sí. ¿Cuál es tu nombre?"

"Eduardo."

"Come on, Eduardo."

Nikki tugged the boy through the hidden hatch. The child was weak and thin, as if he'd spent days in the boat's bowels with no food or water. He could barely move and his skin felt like parchment. Nikki handed him up to Mansfield, who'd called in the mission and was ready to haul refugees onto the deck.

"Ninety miles isn't that long," Mansfield muttered, referring to the nautical distance from Cuba to Miami.

"No," Nikki replied grimly as anger flash-fired in her stomach, "but I'm guessing these passengers weren't meant to arrive."

She kept count as they pulled out man after

woman after child. Her boarding crew, in full-out rescue mode, worked quickly. Still, it was well over an hour to move the refugees out and give them water.

"One last check." Nikki held the flashlight out to Mansfield, who blanched, green around the gills. "There may be more people down there. Are you going to do your job or not?"

Mansfield shook his head.

Nikki tamped down her anger-fueled disgust at his cowardice. "Never mind."

She lowered herself back into the hold and played the flashlight beam over the paint-peeling sides.

"How's it look, boss?" Jackson's voice echoed hollowly in the now-empty hold.

"Gotta do it right."

He grunted as she crawled methodically through the wretched space, which was only three feet high. No wonder the terror had been so great. The shrimper was a death trap—no air circulation, hotter 'n hell, with over a hundred and forty people crammed inside. Toward the stern, the shrimper's internal bulkheads provided too many shadows and too much cover for Nikki to assume they'd found everyone.

The coffee scent still lingered, as it would for several more days. If the emotion was strong enough—the rage or terror or love—it made sort of an imprint, and the stronger the emotion, the clearer and more lasting it was. She concentrated on that smell rather than what was wafting off the floor she crawled across, avoiding puddles and slicks of human bodily fluids. The detritus of desperation.

And to starboard, deep in the stern, Nikki found the girl.

She might have been eleven years old, maybe twelve, huddled against the boat's bulkhead, her jeans stained and her shirt torn. As the light splashed across the girl's face, Nikki was struck by a sense of familiarity. But there was no way she could know this child. She touched the girl's sweat-slickened hand, glad to find her alive. Barely alive.

"Got another one!" Nikki shouted back at the hatch. "She needs a medic!"

Nikki quickly pulled the child into her arms and started the laborious journey to the hatch. Ignoring the wetness seeping through her uniform, she concentrated instead on speed. The girl's breathing was extremely shallow and her cold skin said she was in shock.

It took only a few more moments to lift the child—she weighed so little—into Jackson's arms, then follow him into the pilothouse. Jackson's bulging forearm looked obscenely strong next to the girl's skinny limbs as he laid her carefully on a workbench Mansfield had cleared of clutter.

"Where's the doc?"

"He's got his hands full on deck."

"He needs to be in here," Nikki snapped. "Mansfield! Get the doc in here, now!" And when he hesitated, she shouted, "Don't hang around, ensign!"

Mansfield jerked into gear and headed out onto the deck. Nikki dug through a gear bag for a space blanket, frustrated by the piles of supplies that got in her way. There! Shaking the blanket out, she turned to cover the girl, but Jackson cursed suddenly and started CPR.

"We're gonna lose her!"

Nikki poked her head out of the pilothouse. "Doc! Get your ass in here *now!*"

She spotted the physician and Mansfield in the stern, bent over a woman whose arms flailed in some kind of delirious panic. Dammit.

"Lieutenant." The desperate edge in Jackson's voice brought her back. "She's not going to make it."

"She will. Keep working."

"No, she won't. Her chest is too damaged." Jackson pressed two thick fingers to the girl's carotid artery. "She's gone."

Nikki said nothing. How could she? There was nothing to say. She simply straightened the girl's flimsy, once-white shirt and folded her arms over her stomach. Only then did Nikki see the bruises that necklaced her throat, spread across her collarbone and shoulders and blossomed beneath the blouse.

"Crushed," Jackson murmured. "Internal damage mostly."

"Wave action probably aggravated it," Nikki said. "All that banging around down there. All the people."

Do I know this kid? she wondered. The shape of the brow, the high cheekbones, the soft, full lower lip. The sense of near recognition was strong but Nikki couldn't quite make the connection.

She mentally shook herself and held a tight rein on her frustration. She had work to do. She snapped her own jumpsuit straight and, leaving Jackson with the girl, headed out on deck.

"How many?" Captain Pickens barked as he came aboard. *Undaunted* had been lashed alongside the trawler and now nodded serenely, her boarding bridge deployed.

"One hundred and forty-one living." Nikki's throat tightened. "Three dead."

"How long have they been at sea?"

Anger came to a sudden boil in her stomach. "A man I questioned said three days." Nikki was about to scrub her face with her hand, then caught a whiff of her fingers and stopped. "The fatalities were caused by the crush. Rough seas."

Captain Pickens swore eloquently before saying, "Chopper's on its way for the deceased."

Nikki nodded.

Only the poorest chanced the ninety-mile crossing from Cuba to Florida in an open boat. Anyone who could scrape together a few hundred dollars bought transport aboard fishing trawlers like the *Montoya* or, if they had enough cash, in cargo planes that touched down on small private landing strips near the Everglades. No matter how the journey was made, it was always dangerous.

Nikki glanced around. On the shrimp boat's deck,

the refugees who hadn't been escorted to the *Un-daunted* sat crammed together in little groups, their clothing matted and sweat-darkened. The fear stench on deck had waned but beneath it lay the thicker musk of dread. They'd been caught at the edge of United States territorial waters. After processing, they'd likely be sent back, their life savings forfeited on a failed chance at a better life.

What would she do if she were in these refugees' place? she wondered. Spend her savings for a one-way ticket to another country? Risk everything to cross the Florida Straits? Put her life in the hands of men who might take her out into a desert somewhere and kill her for the fifty dollars she carried, or who thought she was attractive enough to sell to the highest bidder?

Then she made the connection. The girl's face, her features—they looked like the girl in the ancient photo her mom used to pull out and show her at Christmas. The one of her grandmother, who hadn't survived the trip to a better life, either.

Nikki stifled a sigh, grabbed her clipboard and started the interviews.

Chapter 2

That evening Nikki settled back in her home office desk chair while staring at the e-mail messages coming in. One of them, sent from the mysterious Delphi, churned in state-of-the-art decryption software Dana Velasco had given her. While Nikki waited, she absently finger-combed her curly hair, damp from her long shower.

The dead girl's face still flashed in her mind every so often, taking her unawares—while getting into her Jeep, when she opened her modest town house's front door, while she stood under the pounding hot water. Her job could be a bitch sometimes, not for what she did or had to do, but for what she had to face.

In the meantime, maybe the e-mail from Delphi would take her mind off the girl.

Seconds later, the decryption software spat up a simple message:

> Signal broadcast from 25° 37' 33.94" N, 79° 38' 10.18" W. What vessels passed through these coordinates on April 27 at 4:30 p.m.?
> Stand by for contact.

Nikki sat forward as she read. Decrypted, but cryptic, just like the message back in February about watching her back.

So the signal had come through just two days ago. And that location was definitely within her jurisdiction, in the commercial shipping lanes just outside the Port of Miami. Ever thorough, she double-checked the lat-longs against the navigational chart hanging on her office wall for confirmation.

Staring at the chart's looping blue depth lines, she frowned. Dozens of container ships, tankers, cruise ships and tugs passed through those lanes on their way to and from the Port of Miami every day. That bay was heavily trafficked at all hours.

Fortunately, she knew just who to tap. Two-Finger Jimmy owed her a favor or three. Time to pay up.

Nikki flipped through her mental Rolodex and pulled up Two-Finger Jimmy's pager number. Jimmy Delano worked on the clerical side of the Port of Miami, which meant she and Jimmy went back a couple of years comparing notes on port traffic for Homeland Security. Last year she'd spent her off-hours helping him track down his niece, who had disappeared in Little Havana. After a week of searching, they'd found her on a ritzy yacht anchored near South Beach. She'd had a heroin buzz and a nasty case of VD. Considering she was only fifteen, the authorities had not looked kindly on the sleazy television producer who'd introduced her to high-dollar whoredom under the guise of making her a star.

Within minutes, Two-Finger Jimmy's number flashed on her ringing cell.

"James!" she said.

"What have I done now?"

"It's what you're going to do for me."

His voice dropped, got husky. "You know what I'd *like* to do for you."

Nikki laughed. Two-Finger Jimmy had a jockey's physique, was happily married to a woman roughly the size of a wall and was old enough to be her grandfather. "Yeah, I do know. You'd like to look through the port logs for a vessel that might have passed through a waypoint I'm going to give you."

Jimmy chuckled. "That's second on my list. How've you been?"

She shot the breeze with him for a few minutes before cutting to the chase and giving him the lat-longs and date and time information. "Think you can track down the ships that might have passed through those coordinates?"

"Are you kidding? I have technology on *my* side. You're still filling out forms in triplicate, aren't you? On a Smith-Corona?"

"Screw you," Nikki retorted good-naturedly.

"Why, look here, *chica,* I've got the goods."

She grabbed a pen and pulled a legal pad close. "Hit me."

"You've got two ships going out and one ship coming in that could have hit that waypoint around that time. The one coming in was an oil tanker out of Saudi."

"Talk to me about the ones going out."

"One's Maersk-Sealand—their regular shipment. The other's an outfit called 'SHA.' S. H. A."

"What were they carrying?"

"You don't ask much, do you?" Two-Finger Jimmy huffed but Nikki also heard the speedy clicking of the typing technique that had earned him his nickname.

"Maersk-Sealand was routing long-haul trucks to Australia."

"Sounds reasonable."

"SHA was…" He trailed off, then grunted. "It's hard to tell what these clowns were shipping. *Uno momento.*" His off-key whistling set in.

Not a good sign. It meant he was puzzled, and a puzzled Two-Finger Jimmy usually meant trouble.

"Textiles," he said finally. "Handwoven."

"Textiles?"

"Ye-a-ah." He drew the word out nice and slow. "Big bolts of cloth."

"I know what textiles are, James. Aren't they going in the wrong direction?"

"Most textiles come in, but we do ship out occasionally. Problem is, this is about a half load."

"Doesn't sound very cost-effective."

Jimmy grunted. "It's not. SHA's losing its ass on that container ship."

"Nothing but big bolts of cloth?"

Keys clicked. "Nothing that shows on the electronic manifest. Hang on. Let me check the hard copy." Papers fluttered. "Okay, a last-minute load. One container."

"Contents?"

"Not listed." Jimmy whistled. "Someone at SHA has been a ba-aa-ad boy. All container contents are s'posed to be logged and checked by customs twenty-four hours before loading. Looks like this one got loaded up after the rest of the ship's containers were inspected."

"Could that container have bypassed a customs inspection?"

"Only if money changed hands somewhere down the line."

"Sounds like a snakehead's involved," she said.

"Human smuggling? Stowaways usually try to get in, not out."

"True." She thought for a moment. "What do you know about SHA?" she asked as she used Google to search the company name.

"They log about six, seven shipments a year.

Small scratch. Manifest says they have offices in Hong Kong, Singapore and Istanbul."

"Where's this boat headed?"

"Itinerary says Hong Kong. Should take about four weeks to get there."

Four weeks from April 27 meant the container ship would be in port in less than a month, give or take the weather.

Then a thought occurred to her. "Were any civilian passengers logged for this trip?" Sometimes adventurers would book passage on a commercial shipper as an alternative to flying. The signal Oracle picked up might have originated from a passenger.

Jimmy rummaged on the keyboard for a moment, then said, "One guy. An Alexander Wryzynski."

Nikki scribbled down the name as he spelled it for her. "Thanks for the trouble, Jimmy. I owe you."

"Anything for you, *chica,* anytime." He clicked off.

Nikki's smile faded as the search engine came up with about twenty-eight thousand incomprehensible listings for SHA.

SHA, she discovered, was a database programming tool used to encrypt data, so the vast majority of the search links led to either propeller-head sites or to database companies. Including *shipping, transport* and *China* in the search term brought up more programming links, only in Chinese.

The manifest had listed the SHA company as based in Hong Kong, with offices in Singapore and Istanbul. She tried a search with those cities and *shipping,* and dropped *SHA.* Bingo. A plethora of shipping companies, none of which were SHA. What shipping company these days didn't have a Web site?

So a little-known shipping company had sent a light load of handwoven textiles in the least likely direction for such goods to go, and taken on a single container of unknown contents that had bypassed U.S. Customs and Border Control.

It smelled as rotten as the shrimp she'd raked this morning.

Nikki blew out a breath. She had her mark. She fired off two words via e-mail to Delphi: *Got it.* Now she'd just wait to be contacted.

Delphi's e-mail warning back in February had been followed up by a face-to-face visit from a former classmate, Dana Velasco. Dana had been two years ahead of Nikki and now test-piloted experimental planes for a major aircraft manufacturer. Oracle, Dana had told her, was an intelligence-digesting system run by someone known only as Delphi.

"I don't know who Delphi is," Dana had said over a crowd of lively teenagers as they walked down Calle Ocho in Little Havana, "but they've used Oracle to piece together puzzles intelligence agencies can't manage on their own."

"And Athena figures in how?"

Dana had only shrugged. "A lot of what gets pieced together has to do with the academy. And students like you."

Students like you. Nikki sighed and kicked back in her office chair. Students like her, who'd been manipulated at the genetic level, unbeknownst to their parents.

Jaime and Teresita Bustillo hadn't wanted much—just a girl. Seven sons had kept their upscale East Flagstaff construction business going, but they'd wanted one last chance at a daughter. That's where the fertility clinic in Zuni, New Mexico, came in. The clinic, doctors assured her parents, could guarantee a girl.

They just hadn't mentioned that the girl, conceived in vitro and implanted in her mother's womb, would be born with a little something extra. That little secret would be kept until only a few months ago, when Delphi made her phone call and Nikki finally understood the details about where her "gift" had come from. Nikki, Delphi had made clear, wasn't the only girl to have a special talent.

Another, Nikki knew immediately, was her best friend, Jessica Whittaker. Jess had been two years ahead of Nikki at the academy, but *something* had drawn them together. Maybe it was the fact they were both "egg babies," even though they, at the time, had had no idea why they could do what they could. Maybe it was that Jess seemed like the older sister Nikki didn't have. Whichever, as Nikki had grown up at Athena Academy, she'd found herself closer to Jess than even to her Hecate sisters.

Egg baby. Jess could breathe water and Nikki had

a nose like a bloodhound. It was almost as if the scientists at Lab 33 had been splicing in the traits that humans longed for but didn't have.

Which often made Nikki wonder if Catwoman really did exist out there. Or someone more brutal, more cunning, more…insane.

Her cell buzzed and Nikki caught it on the second tone. "Bustillo."

"Girlfriend!"

"Dana!" Nikki replied, grinning. *"¿Cómo estás, chica?"*

"Hell, Nik," Dana groaned. "My Spanish still sucks, okay?"

"You said you were going to practice."

"Life's short but the journey's busy. Let's eat."

"Name the place."

"That little club we didn't get to check out last time I was there. In a half hour."

Nikki hung up. The little club they'd missed was called Hoy Como Ayer, a few blocks away, and it deserved something much nicer than her gray sweatpants and a ragged T-shirt. She dug through her closet until she came up with a red knit top and a short black skirt with a bit of flare to the hem.

Twenty minutes later Nikki sat in a corner table as far away from the little stage as she could get. A couple of youths unloaded gear from a lowered pickup truck outside; Thursday nights jammed with class acts from the finest musicians and singers working the circuit. According to Nikki's watch, she had five minutes to wait for Dana and another hour before the night's live music would start.

On the dot, Dana wound through the growing throng toward her table. Dressed in a flowing, flowery skirt and a solid black top, her dark hair loose on her shoulders, Dana looked striking—and totally unlike a *turista.*

"Hey, girl," Nikki said as she rose to hug Dana.

"Have you heard from Jess?" Dana asked casually as she pulled out a chair.

"Not since a phone call before she left on vacation." Nikki put a not-so-slight emphasis on *vacation.*

Dana's impassive face said as much as Nikki had guessed already: Jess wasn't on vacation, but doing something that was no doubt extremely dangerous. For the same Delphi that had contacted Nikki in February? Because she and Jess were both targeted for kidnapping because of their genetic mutations?

"Have *you* talked to Jess recently?" Nikki asked. As former classmates in the same year, Dana and Jess might have kept in contact more frequently than even Nikki and Jess, though Nikki doubted it. Her surrogate big sister always stayed in touch. Even when she had to be coy about what she was up to, like in their last conversation.

Dana shook her head as a waiter arrived. "No, I haven't heard from her. What's a *mojito?*"

"Better than a kick in the head," Nikki muttered, irritated that Dana was being close-lipped about their mutual friend.

"I'll have a *mojito*," Dana told the waiter.

"Agua," Nikki said to him.

"Spoilsport."

Nikki merely nodded. They both knew Dana would take a sip, maybe two, from her drink and then leave the rest. Dana couldn't afford to be off her game when she was on duty.

Whatever *on duty* meant for her.

After they ordered, Nikki grabbed a baked plantain chip and hit the spicy guacamole with it. "What's up?"

"You found what we're looking for."

"Maybe." Nikki relayed the information she'd gotten from Two-Finger Jimmy and finished up with, "So the SHA shipment to Hong Kong looks like the one you want. It's carrying a passenger and a suspicious cargo container."

Dana waited until the waiter served their drinks and left.

"Sounds like you've pegged it." Dana sipped the *mojito*—a concoction of rum, lime juice and mint, among other things—and smiled broadly. "Can I get this to go?"

"Not in this town. What's going on with the container ship?"

Dana twirled the mint sprig in her drink. "Athena needs you to track it. It has something we want."

"Athena needs it?" Nikki frowned. "Is this related to our kidnapping conversation from a couple of months ago?"

"I can't say." Then after a moment, Dana added, "I'm not authorized."

Nikki's frown deepened but she couldn't suppress the urge to lean on her friend. "Is it related to Jess's vacation?"

Dana said nothing.

Nikki cursed inwardly. Dana's silence meant *yes,* but the woman would never say. "Look, you can't expect me to keep running your little errands without telling me something of what's going on. I'm in danger, Jess is in danger." And when her friend still kept quiet, Nikki added, "Throw me a bone here, Dana. Give me something or I walk."

Dana leaned back in her chair, her face immobile, as if considering.

Nikki, thoroughly annoyed, tossed her napkin on the table. "Are you talking or am I walking?" She felt a slim satisfaction when Dana leaned forward.

"Last time we talked face-to-face, I told you about Arachne."

"Yeah, crazy woman trying to kidnap Athena students with special talents."

"I didn't tell you that she succeeded. With some Athena students."

Nikki's breath caught in her throat. There was no telling what someone like Arachne might do with genetically modified children. *Children.* Nikki tried to ignore her own fear scent rising in her nostrils. "How many?"

"Two, plus one eager beaver who was instrumen-

tal in our blowing up a Lab 33 wannabe in Kestonia."
Dana's sharp eyes must have picked up on Nikki's
face because she said quickly, "It's okay. We got
them all back, safe and sound."

Relief swept like cool water through Nikki's veins.
It was one thing for this Arachne to try to kidnap a
grown woman, and another thing entirely for her to
target girls. And succeed, no matter how temporarily.

Nikki nodded. "Good."

"But we've had other information come to light and
that's why I'm here. If you're willing to serve Athena."

Nikki's chin lifted as anger swirled in her gut.
Dana knew her better than that. Stung, she retorted,
"There's no 'if' about it. What do you want me to do?"

"The signal we had you track came from someone
called Diviner. We don't know who Diviner is, but
we need him. Or her."

"You're sure the perp is human?" Nikki asked,
thinking of Alexander Wryzynski.

Dana nodded. "We intercepted an instant message, definitely generated by a human. He, or she,
thought he was talking to Bryan Ellis."

"The congressman."

"The congressman who tried to kill Francesca
Thorne two months ago. He's been charged with
conspiracy to commit murder."

"I remember Chesca. I ran into her once on the
firing range." Nikki frowned. "She didn't say much
but I could have sworn her eyes would cut glass.
Like she could see right through me."

"Quiet and thoughtful," Dana agreed.

"And scary," Nikki added.

"Bryan Ellis gave us Diviner as part of his plea bargain. When we made contact, we came away with the signal location, but that was all. I'll look into Wryzynski. That's the best lead we've got."

"Where do I come in?" Nikki asked.

Dana pitched the straw into her drink and settled back. "Care for a trip to Hong Kong?"

Nikki regarded Dana for a moment. "I have leave coming up. Might be able to get a couple of weeks if I ask nicely."

"Then you'll do it."

Dana was all business, even when she was being friendly. She knew about Nikki's origins in Lab 33, just as she knew Jess's. She also worked for the mysterious Delphi, who herself—or himself—was the mouthpiece for the more mysterious Oracle.

And all these pieces came together around the Athena Academy, where Nikki had found herself surrounded for the first time by women. Not just women. Like-minded women who were driven by a sense of purpose, and who weren't afraid to sacrifice whatever it took to achieve a greater good.

Like the people on the shrimp trawler this morning, who'd been willing to sacrifice everything— homes, jobs, community—to bring their children to a foreign land for a chance at a better life. For the greater good of the family.

Nikki knew about the greater good of the family.

She had her own family full of crazy, laughing brothers and loving parents. She had the Hecates and Jess.

She had Athena, which suddenly faced threats against it, threats against its students, past and present.

The waiter placed steaming platters of food in front of them, but neither woman touched her plate.

Nikki's jaw clenched. "Arachne has it in for Athena."

Dana's silence spoke volumes. It just didn't give details.

Nikki nodded, satisfied. For the moment. "Hong Kong."

Chapter 3

The moment Nikki stepped into the Hong Kong International Airport terminal, she turned on the GSM quad-band phone Dana had given her. Not only was Delphi well-informed, Nikki thought, but she provided cutting-edge technology to her field operatives. A built-in scrambler kept messages safe.

Nikki snorted. *Field operative. Yeah, that's me.*

Still smiling, she slung her backpack over her shoulder, preparing to shoulder her way through the throng flowing toward the illuminated sign that read Trains to city. A chirping sound started up and it took her a moment to realize it was her new phone. She slid sideways through the slipstream of travelers to a vacant spot by the wall.

Nikki answered the phone with, "Your timing's good."

"There's a problem," Dana replied. "We lost your contact."

Nikki settled her backpack between her feet. "What do you mean 'lost'?"

"Regina Woo's been killed."

Shock coursed through Nikki's veins as she let her back make contact, hard, with the polished stone wall. She didn't know Regina—she was another Athena student who'd graduated before Nikki arrived—and had had limited contact with her to set up their meeting, but…she was Athena. She was a sister. And having grown up in Hong Kong before moving to the States, she was a natural contact for this mission to find Diviner.

"What happened?" Nikki asked.

"She was ambushed leaving work late last night. It looks like a gang murder to the police, but we think the gang was reporting to someone else."

"Who?"

"Triads."

Well, hell. Nikki knew of the triads only by reputation. The gang specialized in cocaine and heroin export with side businesses in extortion and child prostitution. They also had a nasty habit of cutting off the fingers of members who'd disappointed them and giving a traitor the "Death By a Thousand Cuts."

"What about the guy Regina hired to keep

watch for the SHA vessel?" she asked. "Is he still working for us?"

"As far as we know." Dana was silent for a moment. "Regina worked with several people. Let's hope Johnny Zhao is one of the less…interesting…ones."

"I don't have a way of contacting him. I'll have to meet up with him in port." Nikki cursed inwardly. Meet up with a man whose face she didn't know in a city she'd never visited and without her familiar Smith & Wesson 9 mm in her hand. This didn't look good. Or feel good. She could be walking toward her death just as readily as Regina had. "I don't like it."

"What do you want to do?"

Nikki didn't hesitate. "Finish the job."

"You sounded unsure."

"I was just stating a fact." She lowered her voice as a tourist couple, English by their tweed slacks, walked by, gawking and dragging heavy suitcases. Nikki tried to keep the annoyance out of her voice as she said, "I couldn't bring a firearm into the country and I'm stuck now without a weapon. Or a translator in case this guy doesn't speak English like the rest of post-Brit Hong Kong. I don't like it. These are facts, but they don't mean I won't finish what I've started."

"I might be able to call in some backup from New Mexico—"

"Our window's closing," Nikki snapped. "The ship is due in tonight and I need to be on it as soon as I can get on it. I can't afford to wait for someone else to fly in as backup. Our mark will have disappeared by then."

"You're right."

"I'll hook up with the contact if I can find him and go from there."

"Call me tomorrow." A pause. "If you get a chance."

Nikki nodded. Dana actually meant *if you're still alive.* "Will do."

She snapped the phone shut.

Her first priority was to locate this Johnny Zhao guy, assuming he was still alive. He was supposed to be stationed at the container terminal, but as she didn't know his face, she had no idea who to look for.

It's easy, she reprimanded herself. *Look for the armed Chinese guy in black hanging out in the shadows.*

Right.

This mission would be a challenge, but she'd faced challenges before. Unbidden, the Cuban girl's face surfaced in her mind. She ruthlessly shut the vision out of her head. Time to get moving. The sooner she hooked up with Zhao, the sooner she'd get her hands on a sidearm. Or a rifle. Preferably both.

She headed down the wide tunnel toward the trains, and a huge party of Chinese caught up to her, talking amongst themselves in complex, tonal Cantonese. As they swirled around her, dragging their luggage and waving at small children to catch up, Nikki caught the clean cotton scent of new clothes layered on warm flesh that exuded garlic, ginger and some other scent she couldn't name. They closed around her tightly, enveloping her completely until her wide-open-spaces, American self felt almost claustrophobic, then hurtled forward to close around her as if she were a tree planted in the middle of a stream.

A hard bump knocked her elbow forward. Nikki instinctively rocked onto the balls of her feet, ready to fight.

A little girl in a pleated skirt and crisp white shirt shot her a half-fearful, half-apologetic smile as she sprinted past, her perfectly straight blue-black hair shimmering on her shoulders. A man who might have been the girl's father cuffed her gently and guided her in front of him.

Nikki decided she was a helluva long way from home.

The wind kicked up and the scent hit her face-first: sea and salt mixed with diesel fumes and old fish. Now *this* felt more like home.

Nikki flattened into the shadow of massive metal containers stacked four high and hoped the security guard wouldn't hear the water dripping from her wet suit. He walked briskly, his boots crisp on the pavement, and disappeared down past a line of containers laid out like a child's carefully arranged toy blocks.

The Kwai Chung Container Terminal was a city that never slept. It gleamed at night, lit partly from its own high-powered floods and partly from the high-rises packed along the southwest shore of the New Territories. Of its nine terminals—Kwai Chung was the busiest container terminal in the world— Terminal Eight would accept delivery of the SHA shipment.

And it had taken a heckuva lot of cunning to get inside. Fortunately, no one had been watching the water for sneaky swimmers. The ladder bolted into the concrete pier was just as convenient for her as it would have been for a clumsy sailor, and the metal gate guarding it had yielded to some basic lock-picking.

Her goal was simple. Get aboard the SHA vessel and use her PDA to scan for a signal. If Diviner was on the ship, the signal strength would lead her to him. Then she'd contact Delphi.

Nikki peeled out of her wet suit to reveal a black long-sleeved shirt and the formfitting black pants she used for her martial arts training workouts. Her face she'd already smeared with grease, and her hair was swept back in a secure ponytail. The waterproof gear bag was slung on her back like a backpack.

She glanced around the corner of the container stack that hid her. The SHA vessel loomed at the pier's edge, its massive dock lines—as big around as her waist—looped over the equally massive mooring cleats. Lights blazed on deck as dockhands moved back and forth, adjusting lines and checking the payload. A man in a hard hat and carrying a clipboard emerged from the bridge tower, shouted something to the workers, then headed down the boarding plank for the dock.

Getting aboard that vessel wouldn't be anywhere as easy as getting into the terminal.

It would have helped if she'd been able to find Johnny Zhao, but he either wasn't around or he was a ghost. She just hoped he wasn't the kind of ghost who started out alive but was now dead. Or the kind of ghost who turned on his employer, killed her and then faded away.

Anger mingled with fear trickled through her muscles. If he'd killed Regina Woo—and if she could find him—she'd have his hide.

Nikki waited until she counted eight men leaving the vessel. If whatever was on board was important, it'd likely have security teams crawling all over it. She saw only one man still on deck, a pistol holstered at his belt, so perhaps the ship was running a skeleton crew.

The terminal's security guard made another pass through the stacked containers. Nikki checked her watch. His schedule gave her about ten minutes to get up and out of sight.

She shimmied through shadows until she crouched next to the bow mooring cleat. The huge dock line arced gracefully up to the vessel's scupper; the nearest big floodlight pointed away from the bow. Perhaps her unorthodox entrance would go unnoticed. Either that or everyone would see her grappling for purchase on the way up. Not pretty.

Nikki hopped onto the cleat and tested her footing on the dock line. Her soft shoe soles gripped the rough, twisted line, and its texture gave her plenty of purchase. The good news was that it wasn't anywhere as difficult as dragging herself up a Coast Guard cutter's wave-washed deck in high seas. In moments she had inched her way up to the scupper and hoisted herself over the rail and onto the deck.

Another minute of sticking close to shadows and moving silently had her sequestered near the containers still stacked aboard the ship. Above her, a crane's giant hook hung in the air, abandoned, as if the five o'clock whistle had just blown. On the ship, the containers sat bunched together and tied down by massive cables, with little space for a smallish woman to slide between them. Still, she managed to squeeze in.

Hard-soled boots clanged on the steel deck, driving her deeper into the shadows. While she waited for the deckhand to pass by, she scanned the containers that hid her. Nothing out of the ordinary. She needed to get inside, where passengers—including Alexander Wryzynski—would be awaiting the captain's permission to disembark.

Out of the corner of her eye, she noted a blip of black between the metal containers—someone had passed the gap where she hid. The better place to evaluate the situation would be up top, she realized, and pressing her feet and hands on opposite containers, she crept up between them, using leverage to keep herself suspended. Another blip of movement. Nikki froze. When the person disappeared, she crab-walked the rest of the way to the top.

Far enough from the ship's deck lights to be in shadow even up here in the open, she could safely assess the situation.

The ship's five-story bridge gleamed like a Hong Kong skyscraper. She counted six men walking purposefully past windows that were probably crew quarters. Another two, judging from their footsteps far below, paced the deck. Might as well assume another two, maybe three, in the engine room.

Were they all crew, or a security team, or what?

And where the hell was Johnny Zhao? According to her last phone call with Regina, he was supposed to meet them here.

Ten crewmen. One potential but notably absent ally. One unarmed woman.

That sounded about right.

Nikki stifled a snort and pulled her PDA from her gear bag. It fired up instantly.

"Wireless signal, come to mama," she mouthed as she launched the signal probe.

The PDA registered two wireless signals: one from the terminal that looked like a wide area network, and one whose network name was complete gibberish. Not even random numbers and letters, but blocks, as if it used an alphabet unavailable to her PDA.

Is that you, Diviner? she wondered.

Her PDA faithfully monitored the signal without attempting to access the machine producing it. Dana had told her that Oracle believed the signal to be a sophisticated satellite hookup rather than part of a standard network. The gibberish seemed to confirm that.

The mystery signal was pretty strong, seventy-four percent. Nikki scuttled aft, toward the bridge, then paused. The signal strengthened a fraction to seventy-six.

Nikki stowed the PDA back in her gear bag. There was little chance she'd manage to get onto the bridge or into the hold unnoticed. Maybe she should try to arm herself first.

She slipped back between the containers and shimmied down to the deck. Moments of darting between big metal boxes, pausing to check for guards and sprinting across the occasional open area put her beneath the overhang of the bridge's house and once more out of the light. She was ready to go inside, and the starboard door sat invitingly open about six feet away.

Shouts drove her to drop to her knees. A split second later, a bullet pinged off one of the containers. She lunged for the bridge door and spun around it—

And stopped short.

The guard's eyes widened. Without thinking, Nikki swept her right arm down to block the gun hand he was raising, then snapped a front kick to his kneecap. It crunched. He went down. She snatched the firearm from his loosened grip, then threw all of her one hundred and twenty-five pounds behind a left cross to his cheek.

This guy weighs more than he looks, she thought as she dragged his unconscious body behind a mess of old tarps. She checked the weapon. A semiautomatic of undetermined make, though she suspected it might be a bootleg QSZ-92 liberated from the People's Liberation Army. Eleven rounds out of fifteen.

The room was a storeroom from the looks of the gear thrown every which way. A single door led deeper into the bridge. She listened hard, but when she heard nothing on the other side, she opened it.

The scent hit her hard, the wet-penny smell of anger, the burnt coffee of terror. Concentrated, it nearly exploded in her nostrils, cloying and acidic.

What had happened here?

Nikki suppressed a cough and breathed through her mouth. The scent was concentrated from the small, dimly lit space, but several days old. Had it been fresh it would have put her on her ass for sure.

She'd ponder this one later, when she had time. Heart pounding from adrenaline rush, she slammed the door shut.

Outside, a man's panicked cry was cut short.

Nikki thumbed the safety off the 9 mm and slipped back outside. It was a regular pattern: men would yell, go quiet, then guns armed with silencers would spit. Almost like they were hunting someone.

Or someone was hunting them.

The coffee smell was starting to be so strong, she thought a pot was brewing under her nose. No time to be scared, she reminded herself.

Nikki ran back to the stern and nearly tripped over a wounded crewman lying half-in, half-out of a pool of deck light. He screamed, shielding his head with his hands. Nikki quickly frisked him but found no weapon. Only a flesh wound in his thigh.

She tucked the semiautomatic in her waistband and tore a strip off the man's untucked shirt.

He lowered his arms. "You American!"

"Do you speak English?"

The man nodded warily. "You've come to rob us."

"Not exactly." She ran the strip underneath his injured leg and cinched it tight above the wound. "What's going on?"

"We are doing our job."

"What job?"

"Guarding the ship."

She knotted the strip and sat back on her heels. "Who's shooting at you?"

"Triads."

Nikki bit her lip. "These triad guys. Can they be identified by what they wear?"

He shook his head.

"Great. I bet there's no secret handshake at the clubhouse, either." At his puzzled frown, she said, "Forget it. Listen, where's your passenger?"

The guard looked confused again. "I don't know. We guard the ship from robbers. We're not crew. That's all."

Well, hell. So much for getting information the easy way. "Stay put and don't move." She started to leave, but thought better of it. Instead, she leaned toward him and said softly, "I wasn't here."

And suddenly, lemons.

Nikki sprang back and to the side. A knife whisked out of the darkness, caught the injured guard in the throat. She pounced. She grabbed the assailant's wrist, still outstretched from his throw, and twisted down toward his body. He bent forward, his elbow locked up. She saw him winding up for a sweep-kick. As it approached, she palm-heeled his vulnerable elbow. The snap was followed by a grunt of pain, and the kick lost its momentum. She applied more pressure to his wrist, driving him face-first to the deck.

After that, it was dealer's choice.

She chose the choke hold. In moments he'd passed out. She liberated another sidearm and a throwing knife. This guy she left in the open. His lemony triumph, always a sign of arrogance, had given him away before she saw him.

Nikki drifted into the shadows on the starboard side again, following the sound of the screams. They grew less loud, less frequent, as she threaded between containers. By the time she reached the bow, silence.

Somebody had made mincemeat out of the triads. Or the guards. Or both.

Nikki settled into a ball on the deck, making herself small and unhumanlike in shape to the careless glance. She eased the gun from her waistband. Then she took a long and careful sniff.

Nothing.

No coppery anger or coffeeish terror. No citrus triumph. Just sea air and diesel fumes wafting over the water.

It felt really, really wrong.

She adjusted her grip on the gun, consciously relaxed each major muscle. Loose, she thought. Stay loose.

In the silence, she finally heard the distinctive scrape of metal on metal, something unscrewing.

A silencer being removed. Or attached.

It was now or never, while he was distracted.

She leaped from between the containers as he spun to face her, her arm outstretched, pistol up and pointed into the man's impassive face. *Gotcha!*

Only she was looking down the barrel of his gun.

Chapter 4

They eyed each other warily. Arms straight and stiff, guns unwavering, muzzles nearly pressed to cheeks.

Nikki forced herself to look past the gleaming barrel and into the eyes of the man who held her life in his trigger finger. In the shadows and half-light, wrapped in some sort of black fighting garb, he was every inch the dark warrior. He looked exactly like the kind of man who could take out well-armed guards, instill terror in grown men and kill without mercy.

His eyes, the only part of his face not concealed by his disguise, were black, calm.

No wonder I couldn't smell him, she thought. He's at peace.

Of course he's at peace, another part of her retorted. He's got two guns.

One aimed at her face, the other at her heart.

Nikki counted breaths. One thousand one, one
thousand two, one thousand three. Lungs full, her life
about to end, she remembered sunlight slanting down
onto Athena Academy's grassy courtyard and the
neighing of the smelly horses she hated to ride. She
thought of the dry dirt and mesquite surrounding the
silver mine where she first truly understood what
her gift could mean, when she'd smelled burnt coffee
and then heard a scared girl's voice echoing up
through the earth.

She'd come all this way just to die.

A tendril escaped from her messy ponytail and
arced down onto her forehead. The heady scent of
fish wafted over the ship's bow. If she listened carefully, she could hear the distant traffic—small cars
and buses darting through heavy weekend traffic.
With one long, slow sniff, she knew the vehicles'
diesel and gas fumes and the rotten eggs of a spent
catalytic converter.

But from her killer, nothing but a hint of ginger
and something akin to warm chalk.

"Can we talk about this?" she found herself saying.

His eyes remained unchanged and he didn't
speak.

She slowly stepped to her right, out of the horse
stance that was starting to burn her thighs. He pivoted
with her. Their guns remained aimed, deadly. She

needed to get close enough to a railing to jump. Maybe in the dark he wouldn't be able to hit her. With either gun. Right.

She backed up a step. He followed.

He stood now in a patch of dim light slanting down from the ship's bridge. He seemed fuzzy, insubstantial. Almost like a ghost.

Her ghost?

"Johnny?" she chanced.

"You are of the goddess?" His lips and tongue made the plain English words sound exotic, slightly thick.

"Athena sent me, yes."

His body betrayed no sudden tensing, no anxiety. If he was nervous, annoyed, or inwardly jumping for joy, Nikki couldn't tell. His guns stayed steady, but his gaze flicked over her formfitting training pants and top. "You are very small."

So are you, she wanted to retort, but didn't. True, she was a little short—it made squirming through boat holds easier—but he wasn't *that* much taller. Her automatic comparison of his physique to Jet Li's might be unimaginative, but it was also accurate.

"The goddess sent more than one emissary," she replied, but couldn't keep the scorn from her voice when she added, "A taller one, no doubt."

His right eye tightened at the corner. Was he laughing at her? Angry? Confused by the English word *emissary?* The wind shifted slightly and she caught the scent of a classic novel she'd picked up once in the Athena library. The copy had been decades old, with yellow, mildewed pages she'd been happy to bury her nose in.

It was the scent of regret.

"My contact said you were of the dark goddess. The dog. Not Athena. Heck-a-tee."

Nikki smiled despite herself. "Yes. Hecate."

"Is that the dog goddess's name?"

"Are you Johnny Zhao?" she countered.

He inclined his head in something like a formal bow, his eyes never moving from her face. Still not trusting her.

"What happened to Regina?"

He abruptly dropped his gun hands to his sides. "An ambush outside her work."

"You were there?"

"I wasn't alert." Zhao flicked on the safeties of both guns and disappeared them into the folds of his fighting trousers. "I let her out of my sight."

"I doubt that was the problem."

"She was my responsibility."

"*She* hired *you*. I'd say that makes things work the other way around."

His eyes narrowed. Nikki wished he'd lose the ninja garb because she wanted to see the rest of his face, not just hear his voice emerging from black gauze. But she didn't need to see him to know that the regret was now rolling off him in waves. He was telling her the truth. He'd felt protective of Regina, that was clear in the light pine underlying the old paper scent. And he'd failed.

Nikki realized she was still holding the semiautomatic on him. She lowered it and was immediately surprised by how strained her shoulder felt. Damn heavy gun.

"Who ambushed her?"

"I don't know yet. It was a professional hit. No clues and no calling cards."

"Did she give you any information I can use?"

Zhao shook his head. "She told me only to keep watch over this vessel when it came into port."

"I can do that now."

"With my help."

His matter-of-fact statement struck her speechless for a moment, then she said, "Maybe."

"Honor demands I complete the mission."

"Do you even know what the mission is?"

The corners of his eyes crinkled. Nikki knew that underneath his makeshift ninja costume he was likely smiling. She wished suddenly she could see his lips, and not to read them for tension or intent.

"I know you will need help. I am commissioned to complete the task. I'm responsible for—"

"Don't," Nikki said around her tightening throat. "She's gone. Let's move on."

"I'm doing that. She paid me for a mission and I will complete it."

Nikki recognized the universal male "ain't gonna budge" look in his stance. Growing up with seven brothers was enough to teach her when she needed to bide her time, and now was that moment. She'd deal with him later, after she had a look around the ship. And since Hero here wanted to come along—and had great stealth skills—she might as well let him.

"What's your background?"

He hesitated and for a moment she thought he'd ignore her question, but he finally said, "Hong Kong police."

She stared. "You're a *cop?*"

He shrugged, as if his occupation was of little interest to him and should be of less to her.

"So you know this vessel belongs to SHA," she pressed.

"SHA is a front for the Wo Shing Wo."

"Who?"

"A triad organization."

Nikki frowned. "A guard I talked to thought the guys attacking the ship were triads. But if he was working for them…"

Her confusion must have been written on her face in capital letters because he said, "Triad means 'mafia.' Different groups inside the mafia fight for control. It's the same with the triads. Hong Kong has more than fifty different factions. Some of them are street gangs. Some are organized. Wo Shing Wo. Fourteen-K. Sun Yee On."

"We've landed in the middle of a gang war. Great."

"There's always a gang war."

She thought she heard fatigue in his quiet voice. She understood. For every cocaine and heroin shipment her squadron intercepted, nine more got through. Sometimes it felt as if it'd never end.

Nikki mentally shook herself. "Which one would likely be trying to hijack this vessel?"

Zhao blew out a breath, making the gauze wrapped around his mouth plume slightly. "Sun Yee On. They've got the upper hand on the streets these days."

"What are they into?"

"The usual. Child slavery, prostitution, drugs. Every vice money can buy." He paused. "They're behind, though."

"Behind?"

"The growth sectors are identity theft and online extortion. It's why the Wo Shing Wo will dominate in another year or two. Markets are changing. The Wo Shing Wo are much more active online."

"Por dinero baila el perro," she muttered. The dog dances for money. "But what are they looking for here?"

"The scouting group was small. How many did you subdue?"

Subdue. Like she'd sung them to sleep. "Two."

"That makes twelve in all. A local group controlling the dockyard. What we need is its red pole."

She looked at him.

"The enforcer in charge," he qualified. "To question him."

"Let's make sure the ship is secured then," she said. "Maybe he's hiding somewhere and I need to have a look around, anyway."

"For what?"

"A passenger who might be the source of a satellite signal." Nikki stuck the semiautomatic in her waistband so she could rummage through her gear bag. She pulled out the PDA and fired it up. The signal was weaker here at the bow but still in the low seventies. Diviner hadn't moved.

"Passengers normally have cabins just below the bridge deck," she continued. "But I don't know how he's getting his signal out through all that metal."

"Let's go look."

She headed back through the cargo containers, slipping easily between them. Zhao followed silently. Aware of him but unable to smell or hear him, her hackles rose. She felt like a mouse being stalked. In moments they'd arrived back at the door where she'd surprised a guard.

Nothing moved inside, so her first victim was still out cold. When Zhao slipped around the corner and headed toward an inset doorway, clearly expecting her to follow, Nikki tried to shrug off her annoyance. He'd been all over this vessel before she'd even shown up; no sense in getting bent out of shape over his take-charge attitude.

A good leader uses all the resources at her disposal, she reminded herself. *Even if it means following sometimes.* The thought still rankled.

In moments they'd threaded through crew recreation quarters littered with porn magazines, tools and mechanical devices broken open for repair, and headed up onto the second deck. Nikki checked the PDA. The signal was dampened within the steel house. The bridge structure acted as a giant Faraday cage, creating enough radio interference that a signal couldn't enter nor leave. It was why radio antennae were mounted outside the house.

And why it didn't make sense that Wryzynski, or Diviner, or whoever, would be generating that satellite signal from inside.

The second-floor galley and dining area was empty but for the three subdued triads Zhao had left there. The third deck's whitewashed hallway ought to have been lit, but only a dim stairwell light gleamed from the far end. Several closed doors lined the hall, their inset jambs creating darker shadows that marched at regular intervals down both sides. They quickly searched each cabin, but came up empty.

Zhao was nearly through the doorway to the bridge deck when she caught the burnt coffee. She tapped his arm. He stopped instantly. She waved him back into the narrow metal stairwell, surprised when he obeyed.

Someone ahead, she motioned.

His dark eyes studied her for a moment and Nikki was suddenly thrown back years, staring into her best friend's eyes while they stood at the mouth of an abandoned silver mine near the Athena Academy's desert campus. Nikki had just equated the scent of burnt coffee with a child's fear, fear that emanated from the bottom of the mine shaft. The experience had left her physically ill, weak and retching. Her claim to knowing someone was lying down that shaft had sounded crazy even to Nikki at the time, but Jess had simply prepared to rappel into the shaft.

Jess had believed her experience was real; she'd trusted her to do what had to be done.

Something like that trust was reflected in Zhao's eyes now.

Nikki motioned toward the doorway. She reached for the L-shaped handle and paused, aware that Zhao suddenly had semiautomatics in both hands. In the half dark, she could see only the outline of his head and the fabric covering the bridge of his nose. She was struck by his stillness, by how he emanated nothing—no scent, no pent-up energy, no aggression. The guardsmen she worked with exuded machismo and nervous energy in the moments before action, but Zhao seemed almost absent from her psychic space.

She'd love to know how he did that. Her own nerves whined like a dentist's drill.

He was waiting for her to make a move.

Nikki inhaled, drawing the air deep into her diaphragm for strength. A heartbeat, then she twisted the knob and jerked the door open to expose the darkened bridge lit only by ghostly green and orange instrument lights.

A bullet winged high and pinged off the metal doorjamb. She dropped and rolled inside. Almost immediately she crashed hard against something that gave—a man's legs. He cried out as he went down. His gun exploded in her ear and clattered on the floor. She shoved him off her prone body and sprang up to straddle his torso. He struggled like a landed fish but stopped when she pressed her pistol's nose to his cheek.

A click and overhead fluorescents glared. Nikki's assailant lay cowering beneath the pistol's muzzle, hands spread wide. The dull gray coveralls spattered with grease said he worked aboard. His frenetic gaze said he was panicked.

She leaned on the gun, pressed its muzzle into his cheek. "Don't move!" she shouted.

The man started shouting back, spittle flying from his lips. What was he saying? His arms flailed, hitting her randomly and hard. She struggled to get her knee on his elbow, then had to defend against a sudden strike toward her neck.

"Help me out here, Zhao!"

A black-booted foot pinned the man's windmilling arm to the floor and a flood of lilting, diving words spilled from Zhao's mouth. The man beneath her abruptly quit fighting.

Nikki, breathing hard, warily leaned back, though she kept the gun on her assailant. "What the hell did you say to him?"

"That you are a crazy American woman and I

cannot control you, so he should be still before you lose your mind and kill him."

"Great."

"What?" he asked as he retrieved the man's gun from the floor. "It worked."

Nikki caught the scent of freshly cut grass. Zhao was teasing her.

She let her smile freeze into a grimace and leaned again toward the man she sat on. He turned his face away, clearly afraid now.

"You're right," she admitted. "What does he know?"

Zhao spoke at length with him. During the exchange, she heard Wo Shing Wo mentioned several times, then the conversation seemed to get darker. Wet pennies emanated from Zhao and the man seemed to be trying to make himself smaller, as if afraid of being struck.

"What's going on?" she asked after Zhao stopped speaking.

He turned toward her then and she saw beneath the black gauze the hard planes of his face. "This man manages one of the Wo's operations. He's the Chou Hai—a liaison officer."

"Yeah. And?"

Zhao's tone was stiff. "He is to prepare this boat to go to Vladivostok with its cargo."

"Of what?" *And why do I have to keep prompting you?* she thought. *Cooperate with me.*

Angry copper surrounded her, nearly stealing her breath.

"Children. For sex slaves."

"Damn pervert," Nikki snarled. She grabbed the front of the man's coveralls in her fist. "Full cargo? How many children is that?" Her voice rose. "Dozens? Hundreds? How many? Tell me!" She shook him hard, then shoved him back against the floor, away from her as if he stank.

In fact, he did. Mostly of fear. But not of shame or remorse.

Johnny's hand covered her shoulder. "It's a large operation. The mainland has plenty of unwanted girls to sell to the highest bidder." His voice was hard and low. "We'll shut these bastards down right now." He then said something to the man, who covered his face with his hands.

Nikki guessed Johnny didn't have to flash his badge for this guy to know he was in deep trouble.

"What about the passenger?" she asked, pulling herself back to the task at hand.

Another long conversation, and then Johnny said, "He doesn't know anything about who was coming in on this boat."

"But the signal's here. My mark is aboard somewhere."

Johnny shook his head. "A few passengers came aboard, but they left en route. He's very clear about that. The rest is just the loaded containers and the crew to sail."

So was Diviner a crew member? And if he or she was aboard, where?

Frustrated, she yanked open a window hatch, stuck her PDA outside and hit the search button.

The PDA blinked blankly at her.

Diviner was gone.

Chapter 5

The Electric Dragon boomed and throbbed in a city that boomed and throbbed, flashed, chattered, clanged, blared, crashed, hammered, screamed, glittered and whooped.

Nikki had been surreptitiously breathing through her mouth, just to be safe, as she and Johnny walked to the club. The last thing she needed was a migraine from scent overload.

She couldn't complain, though. The Electric Dragon was a Wo Shing Wo lair, and it'd been her idea to leverage the information they'd pulled from the liaison aboard the SHA vessel to get into the club and find out who or what exactly that vessel was carrying. The slave manager—and Nikki shuddered with disgust when she thought about it—hadn't known what the incoming cargo was, no matter how threatening she'd looked. But Johnny's connection to the Hong Kong police meant the law now had a bargaining chip. If they could squeeze that information about Diviner from a Wo putz, they would.

And the slave manager—along with the Sun Yee On soldiers who'd attacked his ship—would just have to sit in the Kowloon holding cell run by one of Johnny's HK police buddies in the meantime.

The club entrance's dragon blew red neon flames against a backdrop of more neon. Nikki wished she'd had her sunglasses. Even now, at nearly two o'clock in the morning, she could have used them against all the light beating on her retinas as she and Johnny walked along the streets of Sai Ying Pun, one of the seedier-looking parts of west central Hong Kong.

When the never-ending crowds pressed against her, she was grateful for Johnny's calming presence. He seemed to have a sixth sense about when to reach for her hand to keep her from being swallowed up and carried away in the throngs still crowding the sidewalks.

Now, he stood before the club's beefy bouncer, one hip cocked in a careless stance, his black leather jacket's lapel kicked up against his neck.

He looked, Nikki thought with a spark of awareness, like a young Chow Yun-Fat—beautiful and masculine, sensitive and tough all at once. Nikki closed her eyes briefly against a vision of the actor sprawled bare-chested on a bed in *The Killer,* and gave herself a mental shake. *You can take him home,* she heard Jess's voice tease her, *but you can't keep him.*

She wasn't sure she dared try to take him home.

Nevertheless, he was definitely the right guy in the right place, she thought as he hooked an arm around her waist and pulled her in close. The bouncer was giving her what Jess used to call the Skanky Eye and saying something to Johnny.

She resisted the urge to glance down at the getup Johnny had given her at his place, where they'd stopped to change clothes and lose the camouflage face paint. She'd wanted to go back to her hotel to pick up her own clothing, but he'd insisted on gearing her out.

All his girlfriends must have been tiny because, even as small as she was, the black leather bustier and black skirt he'd grabbed for her out of a closet came close to being obscene. Good thing he'd had a lightweight wrap to put over her shoulders. She'd felt a passing wave of shame—she was actually more demure than most women her age.

But given the bouncer's admiring glance down the shirt's opening, not to mention the strong scent of sandalwood coming off him, the saucy clothes were a good idea, morals be damned. She looked like someone who might be a prostitute, not someone who could, or would, break his kneecaps. That made for a decent element of surprise.

"Let's go," Johnny said after a few words with the

bouncer. He jerked his head at the much larger man and grinned, leering a little at her.

"Great," she said as she strode through the door. "Meat market, eh, *mal parido?*"

Johnny shrugged, still nonchalant.

Nikki gave up wondering if he knew he'd been insulted and squeezed through the ever-present crowd into the club. This time it was her keeping a tight hold on his hand as they threaded their way to the bar. Once there, Johnny nodded to several angry-looking toughs that Nikki pegged immediately as the kind of guys you didn't hang around with unless you were armed.

She was pretty sure Johnny was armed, but where he kept his guns, she was afraid to wonder. His black leather pants didn't leave room for imagination, much less firearms.

She hoisted herself onto a just-vacated bar stool and tried to ignore the man pressing between her and the guy on the next stool. It was more togetherness than she was used to, or ever wanted to experience, but for the most part her new good friend seemed harmless, more interested in getting his drink and getting back on the dance floor than anything else.

While Johnny spoke with a bartender, she cased the joint.

The Electric Dragon was a happening place, packed to the gills with young men and women writhing to the pulsing beat of a techno pop band whose lead singer's voice could strip paint off walls.

The band was cloistered behind a cage, though it was hard to tell whether that was part of the band's aesthetic sensibilities or for their protection.

The neon was worse inside than out, and the constant movement felt like a visual beating, but Nikki managed to puzzle out a black-painted door behind the cage stage, its outline nearly hidden in shadow.

She glanced at Johnny, who was sliding a shot glass of something clear and no doubt viciously potent in front of her.

He smiled politely, his gaze flicking toward the stage. He leaned forward so she could hear him say, "Yes, I see it."

Just as Nikki was marveling over how in sync they were, he ruined the effect by pointedly staring down her cleavage. Then he pulled her bar stool against him where he stood.

"Relax," he said, rubbing his hand over her back in an almost brotherly way. "We're being watched."

"And that should relax me," she remarked, but masked her nervousness by leveling her gaze on him in what she hoped would appear knowing and sophisticated to a Wo Shing Wo thug.

"Yes, it should. They know who I am." He leaned close. "They know who they *think* I am."

"Undercover work?" she breathed into his neck.

His assent sounded more like a groan than a word.

"What if they *really* know who you are?"

"Then we wouldn't have got in." He leaned back and grinned, cocky as ever. "I'm sorry, though."

"About?"

"Claiming territory." His shrug looked apologetic. His hand, dropping below her waist and resting there, was not.

Her abrupt, unconscious inhale caught a bit of everything: the curious sweetness of burning foliage, the dark musk of hot bodies, the tang of spilled alcohol, a woman's cologne that had worn off her body long ago but still lingered in the air. But it was the strong sandalwood surrounding them—raw sexual attraction—that plucked at her nerves. Problem was, she couldn't tell if it was both of them or just her.

It'd taken her years to learn the difference between a true scent and one that pointed to an emotion. In the deluge of smells around her, the merely physical odors seemed to stop where they were, hanging in the air. The emotional "odors" lingered and teased. In this crush of dancers and partiers, those scents mingled until she found it hard to pinpoint their sources.

The sandalwood was almost overwhelming. Johnny might just be "claiming territory," but he'd provoked a swirl of scent she couldn't place.

"Is that necessary?" she snapped, unnerved at her physical response to his possessive gesture.

"Yes," he replied with the air of a man exercising patience with a child. "These men think nothing of a pretty woman's virtue. I do. Now drink up. It won't affect you." He waited until she sipped from the shot glass to add, "Much."

Nikki set the glass down on the ebony bar in the exact wet circle it had inhabited. He was right. The drink didn't taste of anything; the club must be watering down the booze.

Like most Western-style bars, this one had a mirror stretching the length of the wall. While Johnny stood close and looked over her shoulder toward that black door, she concentrated on studying which of the men pacing the room behind her might be Wo Shing Wo. Didn't most gangs have colors or tattoos or some other signal of their affiliation? What was the point of being in a gang if you didn't *appear* to be part of the group? But then, Johnny had likened them to a loosely connected mafia, so maybe the triads were generally uninterested by the idea of overt affiliation.

These thoughts did nothing to lessen her awareness of the broad hand resting solidly on the curve of her hip. Or of the distinct sandalwood that threatened to choke off her air completely.

That couldn't be just her.

She shook her head slightly to toss her curly hair, loose now and flowing over her bare shoulders, back off her arm. When she did, she caught a flash of gold—a series of studs and rings climbing up the earlobe of the man pressing against her between the stools. He smiled and said something in Chinese, and she did what many people do in a foreign country when faced with words they don't understand: she smiled and shook her head.

The man, apparently encouraged despite her silent protestation, leaned his elbow against the bar and settled in for a chat. He was kind of cute in his blue silk shirt and black jeans, eager to talk with her, but his words were lost to the music. That didn't stop him from openly admiring her thighs in the too-short skirt now hiked almost to her ass where she sat on the bar stool. He reeked of sandalwood.

So it wasn't just her. It just wasn't Johnny, whose reflection in the bar's mirror showed a man interested in watching the girls in their tight tops rub against the men they danced with. Nikki glanced at the dance floor. Where'd she been when torso groping became a legitimate dance move? Wasn't China supposed to be a socially conservative country? Or were things different here in Hong Kong?

Her new friend smiled engagingly and squeezed her leg just above her knee.

Her smile froze. In the split second between registering his touch and her impulse to give the guy an edge-hand to the throat, her survival instinct kicked in. The edge-hand became a girlish swipe at his arm as she said, "Back off!"

He grinned widely and squeezed again, his hand moving higher up her thigh.

No scene, she ordered herself. Make no move that would give the game away. Yet.

Nikki leaned away from her new friend just as Johnny angled his broad shoulders between her and the grabber. His expression's ferocity drove the sensitivity from his face, and Nikki thought he looked ready to bite.

Still, he smelled mostly of soap to her. He was putting on an act to protect her from the guy.

The guy smiled and shrugged. Making nice, Nikki thought.

Johnny was having none of it. He jerked his head toward the door and barked something in Cantonese. The guy drew himself up, as if to square off against Johnny, but suddenly a stocky, middle-aged man materialized from the roiling dancers.

His thin, yellow tie glowed in the black light that strobed onto his navy-blue business suit. A genial smile filled his round face as he spoke quickly to both men in a conciliatory tone.

Johnny made a show of relaxing. Several times during the ensuing conversation he said something like, "Sure," which Nikki remembered from her movie-watching meant "Yes." Her friendly groper started to look a little green around the gills.

The business guy nodded and gave a little shoulder-deep bow to Johnny and then to her. "My apologies for my employee's distasteful behavior," he said. "It will not happen again."

Finally, he frowned at the friendly man, who now faintly resembled a well-whipped dog. The two men headed back to the black door.

Johnny's arm came around her waist again as he turned toward her. "You're brilliant. We're in."

Nikki shrugged. "My mother always thought I

was a prodigy, but even she had to explain things to me occasionally. Care to share?"

"Your little friend is a Sai Gou Zai, a low-level Wo soldier. He's supposed to work security, not admire the patrons." Johnny's gaze lingered on her low neckline before flicking away. "The Red Pole was not pleased."

"Red Pole? The guy in the suit is in charge?"

Johnny nodded. "Of this club, yes. Most of the young men you see standing around are Sai Gou Zai working security." He reeled her in closer and bent to say into her ear, "The security gathering is strong tonight. I think the Fu Shan Chu must be here doing business."

She lifted her cheek from his to ask, but he anticipated her question before she could form the words.

"The Fu Shan Chu is the Deputy Mountain Master. He runs operations in this part of the city."

"Including the port?"

"Perhaps. But he's only a step down from the Dragon Head, the Boss."

"The big cheese," Nikki said under her breath.

"Getting to the Deputy Mountain Master will not be easy. But the Red Pole's honor has been threatened by his soldier's incorrect behavior, so he has offered us a gift to prove he's a good host."

Nikki's eyes narrowed. "A gift. Is your undercover identity that high up the food chain?"

"I dropped a few names and got his attention. Now he must save face and we must accept his hospitality. If you're willing to take him up on his offer, we can get inside and see if the Fu Shan Chu—the deputy—is here."

"Couldn't you just tell the Red Pole that we have one of the deputy's head guys?"

"Red Poles are ambitious men. What if he wants that position for himself?" Johnny shook his head. "No, we go inside, see how the land lies, and then confront the Deputy."

"If he's even here."

Nikki fought down the unease rising in her stomach. It didn't sound right to her—none of it did—but she knew her discomfort might simply have its roots in the unfamiliar situation. Besides, even though she had to rely on Johnny Zhao, she wasn't sure he was being entirely straight with her.

If only the guy put off a consistent scent, she'd know for sure. Only that once, when he'd felt regret for Regina Woo's death, had he emoted in any significant way she could intuit. But it was like he almost didn't exist on some level—personal or emotional—and she couldn't read him like she could everyone else.

Her powerlessness hit her head-on and for the first time in her life, she felt truly afraid for herself. This place, these people who stood too close, their voices and the language the mafia types used, the new customs, the new scents, her not being able to carry a weapon, Johnny's complete lack of scent ninety percent of the time: all these things threatened her feeling of security.

"I need a sidearm," she muttered to herself. Her outfit left room only for the Athena phone in its belt holster and absolutely none for a weapon. She'd kicked herself most of the way to the Electric Dragon for not figuring out a way to carry in her skintight clothing, but it couldn't be helped now.

Besides, she had no other way to get this job done—and help the Athena Academy—except to trust a man she couldn't read. She gritted her teeth in frustration.

Johnny smiled and released her waist to take her hand. "Come. I will protect you."

"Like you did Regina Woo?" she asked, suddenly angry.

His face darkened and she was enveloped in a heady mix of old books of regret and wet pennies of anger. "Come on."

His grip tightened and he hauled her toward the dance floor. Her startled protest was silenced when he spun her in place and clamped her against his hard body amid the writhing dancers. His strength caused fear to flutter lightly in her stomach. "I'm keeping you safe," he growled.

He ground his pelvis into hers as the music swung into an erotic, pounding beat. Of all the things that she associated with "safe," his move wasn't one of them. Around them, dancers who'd been waving their arms and jumping up and down in place paired—or tripled—off.

"You don't understand," he murmured into her

ear as his hands cupped her bottom. "The soldier assumed you were a fair target. I was not doing enough to claim you."

"I'm not a whore!" Nikki bit out.

"No, you aren't. You're a *gwai-poh*. A foreign woman." One hand slipped down to toy with the hem of her skirt, his fingertips brushing her skin as he moved against her. "But we have to convince them that you're my *gwai-poh*. I'm sorry."

His lips, warm—no, hot—on her neck had her body tingling in places she couldn't afford to think about. *You can take him home,* she heard Jess's voice again. *Oh, yes,* Nikki thought. She could definitely take him home.

If she trusted him. Which she didn't.

She pressed her fingers against his back. It was as rock-solid as his chest and abs. The man was nothing but bone and muscle and sinew.

"Make it real," he said against her ear. "How would you dance with a lover at home?"

Nothing like this, at least not in public. She wasn't totally inexperienced—she'd lost her virginity in college—but parading around like this just wasn't her style.

She leaned her chin on his shoulder and through slitted lids looked at the men lining the club's walls and guarding its doorways. Some of them looked bored, but more than one had his gaze glued to her and Johnny.

Fighting down the feeling of being trapped, Nikki

leaned away from him to slip her fingers up his torso. His arms held her lower body prisoner. She curved a hand around his neck and tried to breathe without being overwhelmed by the scents lingering over the dance floor. His hair was remarkably soft.

"Relax," he coaxed.

"Why can't we get on with it?" she asked his collarbone.

"I know you are impatient to find Diviner, but in this we must trust to someone else's timing. The Red Pole will tell us when he is ready to present his gift."

She pulled back to look him in the eye. "What do you think it will be?"

"Drugs, probably." He bent his head to brush the corner of her mouth with his lips. To the spectators, the gesture would look erotic. Then he said, "Can't you smell it?"

Nikki bit back a retort and turned her attention away from how good, how raw, it felt to be held so possessively. Instead, she concentrated on singling out the aromas that filled the space, sifting through the scents of bodies, perfumes and clothing detergents; then through the various kinds of alcohol and fruit juices; and finally past the club itself, the smoke-dampened walls, the scuffed floor, the reek of yesterday's ammonia and citrus-based cleaners.

A sweet, pungent, pleasing scent—like burning leaves—pervaded it all.

Opium.

"When we get inside, stay close to me," Johnny

said in a low voice. "The smoke may affect you even if you do not take a pipe."

Fear spiked in her stomach. "I've never—"

"I know. It is why you must be mine. Otherwise, a soldier or even the Red Pole may decide to take advantage of you when you are…relaxed." He nuzzled her nose. "Forgive me."

His lips were surprisingly soft, sensual, on hers. All the anxiety and tension in her nerves exploded upward, from her stomach to her chest. Unthinking, she opened her mouth and he accepted, his tongue sliding languidly in, taking his time. The hand still cupping her bottom kneaded her gently. He tasted as clean as he smelled, as if he'd just drunk from a pure spring.

Johnny winced as he let go of her and stared over her shoulder. "Showtime."

Nikki turned in his arms.

The Red Pole was headed for them, his face beaming with genuine invitation.

Chapter 6

"I wish to make my apologies," the Red Pole said in English as he led them through the black door. "My associates sometimes lack the judgment their work requires."

He swept his arm out, inviting them into a wide, darkened room. "I am Chan Yunxu, owner of this establishment."

Nikki and Johnny stepped inside. When Chan closed the door behind them, the music that had blasted their eardrums was muted to a rhythmic thumping but nothing more. No screeching singer or whining guitars. Lead-lined doors, Nikki guessed.

"As you can see, we offer a place of rest and entertainment," Chan continued.

There must have been twenty couches, maybe more, spread out in the room, and Nikki felt as if she'd suddenly been dropped into a movie set in turn-of-the-century London. Only a few of the couches were occupied, however, and the fragrant smoke that she'd expected to be as thick as fog simply spiraled up in thin streams from the occupants.

It was a laid-back crowd, tended by slender women in *xi pao*—traditional long, tight silk wraps.

Nikki could barely make out a tangle of limbs and clothing on a distant couch. Another few moments of staring and her brain finally clicked: a woman was "entertaining" a client while he smoked.

"It enhances the sexual experience," Chan said over her shoulder. "I am guessing you have not tried our poppy?"

"No," Nikki replied, but her voice sounded faint.

"Please," Chan said. "Lie down. Enjoy yourself."

Mission accomplished, damn her hypersensitive nose. The secondhand smoke was enough to have her limbs feeling heavy. Nikki felt an urgency to get out of the room and into fresh air, but the urgency called from far away.

"I need to leave," she tried to say, but she wasn't sure anything came out of her mouth.

Johnny's strong arm encircled her and held her up just as she started to sink onto the closest couch. "My apologies," she heard him say to Chan. "She is very sensitive."

"Indeed, you are fortunate," Chan replied.

Was that a hint of a leer she heard in the Red Pole's voice? Did he think she'd "entertain" someone while in this state of lucid half-being or whatever it was?

Nikki was aware she was offended, but that didn't really matter. The feeling would pass, she knew, and right now she just wanted to lie down, preferably somewhere near Johnny Zhao, maybe with him wrapped around her. Or her wrapped around him. Entertaining *him* would be nice.

No, wait. She didn't want that. She wanted to find out who Diviner was and where she could find him. Yes, that's what she wanted. She saw her goal perfectly clearly, about a hundred miles out in front of her. One step at a time. There was plenty of time to track down her quarry.

Her knees collapsed.

She heard Johnny calling her name, then her chin was in his hand. Another hand pried open her eyelids. She wanted to say something, but she was pretty sure all that came out was a whimper.

Johnny and Chan started talking excitedly in Cantonese, and moments later she was being carried through another door and settled into an overstuffed armchair.

It was like being dropped into hell.

The small room's carpeted floor and painted walls were covered in the exact same shade of red. A chandelier hung in golden splendor, casting a bright yellow glow onto the red furnishings. The walls held gilt-framed mirrors that echoed the room back at itself. Everywhere, the scent of opium.

Nikki tried to swallow, but it hurt so much she nearly screamed. Or did scream. She wasn't quite sure, though she was very aware of Johnny shouting—that was shouting, wasn't it?—at Chan. In moments Chan was shouting back.

The room was suddenly full of burly men and most of them were yelling. Johnny was holding his own in the match, addressing himself mainly to a classy-looking guy wearing an electric-blue suit with a matching electric-blue tie. Then suddenly Johnny had assumed the position against the wall and was being frisked by men who didn't seem to mind roughing him up in the process.

Fear crawled through Nikki's stomach and up her throat. If he was armed…

One of the men rifled through Johnny's wallet while another held his face to the wall. Nikki's blood drained like hot lead to her feet. If Johnny was carrying his Hong Kong police badge, they were dead for sure.

She had to get up. Gritting her teeth, she managed to squirm into a straighter sitting position.

"Wait!" she said.

Everyone ignored her. Damn macho jerks.

She took a deep breath that had her head spinning and stood. "Leave him alone!" she shouted.

That got them looking at her.

"Be quiet!" Johnny said against the wall. "You can't bargain with them!"

But it was all so clear. So incredibly, beautifully clear.

"Who's in charge?" she demanded. "Who's the Fu Shan Chu?"

The electric-blue suit detached itself from the pack of men and sauntered toward her. As it drew closer, she fought to keep her eyes wide open, not half-drooped as they wanted to be. The Fu Shan Chu was one good-looking guy, that was for sure, longish hair brushing his collar, strong jaw and cheekbones, sensual lips. He reminded her a bit of Johnny.

"Are you about to do something foolish?" the Fu Shan Chu asked as he stopped near her. His gaze dropped to her chest, sparking her annoyance.

"I'm up here," she said.

A gold pinky ring flashed as he waved off her words. "Yes, but you are there, too."

"And I had a chat with your Chou Hai," she continued, "who told us about a little shipment going out later this week to Vladivostok."

The suit stiffened slightly, then barked in Cantonese. Johnny was abruptly released and shoved over to stand next to Nikki. "What do you know of my Chou Hai?" he demanded. When Johnny started to open his mouth, the suit said, "In English."

Johnny glanced at the guards, who'd apparently skipped their English language classes in favor of beating up the honor students. "We were looking for something aboard your SHA vessel and found a Sun Yee On scouting party crawling over the ship. When we had subdued them, we had a talk with your Chou Hai. We can make sure your Russian shipment will be delivered if you give us the information we're looking for."

The man's face showed no emotion, no surprise. Not even a blink. Behind him, Chan's hands kneaded each other.

"The Chou Hai couldn't supply that information, but you can," Johnny continued. "We don't care about your shipment out. We want to know about the shipment in." He paused. "It will cost you nothing to tell us."

The Fu Shan Chu regarded Johnny for a long moment. He let his gaze rest on Nikki, linger over her bustier, study her legs beneath the short skirt. Nikki suppressed the urge to fidget under his scrutiny and instead lifted her chin, though the movement made her slightly nauseous.

"Nor would it cost me to kill you both now and proceed with my plans—"

"But—" she interrupted, then stopped when the electric suit—the real Electric Dragon—raised a hand as if to strike her. Nikki lifted her chin, ready to take the blow. *Bastardo.*

She was suddenly awash in protective pine, the clean, pungent scent that drove the last of the opium from her lungs and throat.

Johnny's single step between her and the Fu Shan Chu provoked four guards to bolt forward, but the

Electric Dragon turned his threatened strike at Nikki into a warning to his men: back off.

"She needs to learn respect," the Dragon told Johnny. "Of course, she will be more valuable if she does not, for certain men would pay a high price for a spirited woman, especially if her…skills…match her appearance."

Johnny nodded warily, but with a hint of sleaze. "Let us first settle the matter of the Chou Hai and the name I need. Then we will settle on the woman."

Rage spiraled through Nikki's stomach as she registered his words. He didn't mean to give her up, she knew that intellectually, but his cavalier act looked a little too real. It had to be convincing, she reminded herself, but her emotions weren't listening to her logic.

"Or I will simply take the woman after I kill you," the Dragon observed in the same manner a man might suggest an afternoon walk.

A jerk of the Dragon's head had his men swarming over Johnny.

Nikki suddenly saw, with almost preternatural clarity, what had to be done.

She yanked her cell phone from its holster and held it up like a beacon. "Let him go or I bomb the boat."

Bomb must have been a familiar word because the guards paused in their wrestling match with the wiry and slippery Johnny Zhao, who muttered, "Don't say anything! Shut up!"

"Don't tell me my ship is rigged," the Dragon said softly.

"All right, I won't," Nikki went on. "And I won't tell you that your Chou Hai spilled his guts when he thought I was going to kill him."

The scent of clean rain wafted over to her. Johnny was amused by her bluff even as he played along.

The Dragon stood transfixed for a moment before wrenching his attention from her cleavage and spitting, "Coward," in disgust.

Nikki fought the sinking feeling she'd just signed the Chou Hai's death warrant. Could the Dragon reach inside a Kowloon jail and kill him?

"You're lying about the boat," the Dragon said.

Oh, but she knew very well exactly how to sink a vessel. "Good thing the ship isn't double-hulled. I only needed a couple of C-4 bricks strapped to a raw-water intake. And since I disabled the bilge pumps, I'm thinking maybe an hour tops to sink it." She tilted her cell to show him the red light declaring the phone's willingness to send the killing signal and smiled. "You're on my speed dial."

The Dragon stared at her. Behind him, a gilded mirror reflected the gilded mirror behind her, and she and the Dragon marched together on and on and on, facing off into infinity.

"I don't mind the loss of a ship," he said finally.

"But you probably do mind the inquiries that will be made," Johnny said. He no longer strained against the men holding him, but simply leaned forward, as if into a strong wind. "The Hong Kong police won't take long to trace the ship to your Chou Hai, and then to you."

"Worse, the Russians'll be pissed," Nikki added.

She slowly, deliberately, pressed an unprogrammed button on the cell, whose red light obligingly blinked. "The detonator is now armed. If I let go of this button but don't press the abort code within five seconds, it'll blow."

The Dragon's eyes narrowed to consider them both. Nikki fought to control her sense of triumph as she smelled his capitulation. Rancid cantaloupe.

"What name do you need?"

"Release my friend first," Nikki demanded.

The Dragon smiled. "He is my guest. You are my guest. We are fine as we are. What name do you need?"

Nikki shook her head. "Let him go." Then she gave him a below-the-belt shot. "We defended your ship against a dozen Sun Yee On soldiers. You owe us something for that. How do I know you're an honorable man?"

The Dragon's breath hissed between his teeth. He barked a few words. Nikki didn't have to look to know Johnny had joined her; his pine scent enveloped her like the opium had.

Johnny said, "We can restore your Russian shipment. But we want to know what came from the States."

"Your ship carried a passenger called Diviner,"

Nikki continued. "Where did he come from and where is he headed?"

The Dragon glared for another long minute, then snapped his fingers. Chan Yunxu hit a number on a cell phone and handed it over to his boss.

While the Dragon talked in a low voice with whomever was on the other end of the call—a bookkeeper, a shipping clerk, an assassin—Nikki counted her breaths. Each clean breath brought a little more clarity to her conscious brain and a little less clarity to whatever part of her brain had thought it was a good idea to tackle the Chinese version of a Mafioso on his own turf. She shifted her weight nervously, but Johnny leaned in just enough to make contact, thigh to thigh, hip to hip.

Be steady. We're in this together, the message said.

The Dragon snapped his phone shut.

"Diviner was indeed on the SHA ship," he said, "coming from the States and spending twenty-seven days at sea."

"But the passenger who boarded in Miami disembarked before arrival here," Nikki said.

The Dragon smiled the smallest of smiles. "Diviner traveled freight, so to speak."

"Freight?" Johnny's voice sounded almost bored.

"Diviner is a container," Nikki said. Of course it was. The suspicious container that had been loaded up in Miami after bypassing customs.

"Of sorts," the Dragon admitted. "He— It travels within."

"We found no passengers aboard and nothing was off-loaded from the vessel," Johnny said in a low voice to her.

Nikki frowned in consternation. Her probe had registered a signal before she ran across Johnny, and then had registered nothing after they'd interviewed the Chou Hai.

Damn.

Nikki wanted to smack her forehead in frustration over her own idiocy. She'd been looking for a human somewhere on the ship because Dana had confirmed Diviner was human. Nikki had assumed he was traveling *with* the container, not *inside* it. So when the signal died, she assumed he'd left the ship.

Here's a dollar. Buy a clue.

Diviner, whoever or whatever he was, had simply turned off the signal.

She fought down a rising tide of anger at her own stupidity to ask the Dragon, "Where's his next stop?"

He shrugged, his subtle suit pattern glinting in the chandelier light like scales. "We only brought him from the States. Where he goes from here is none of our concern."

"Where did he come from?"

"He arrived in Miami from New York, I believe."

Nikki pondered that one for a moment before she said, "The SHA vessel carried only a half load. I imagine you lost money on that shipment."

The Dragon eyed her while Chan fidgeted. Finally the Fu Shan Chu said, "Diviner paid well."

"Half a shipment's worth?" Johnny interjected. "That must be…what? Hundreds of thousands of dollars?"

The Dragon shrugged. "He wanted to be loaded quickly, on top of the other containers. He paid for the privilege."

Something about the way the Dragon said "paid" caught Nikki's attention. Chan's subtle smirk and the lemon drifting over to her suggested they'd gotten their money's worth.

She took a long, slow sniff.

No, it was more than that. It was triumph, all right, but with a hint of retribution around the edges. Old grudges long festering, now settled.

"Did he pay you in cash?" she asked.

The Dragon let a grin widen his sensual lips. "In information."

"About what?"

The Dragon bristled at Johnny's question. "Nothing of your concern."

"They settled an old score," Nikki told Johnny, then turned back to the Dragon. "How could Diviner, who's been traveling for months, maybe years, in a *container,* possibly know enough about your enemies to help you get revenge?"

Surprise registered in the air. Surprise that she'd guessed Diviner's payment? That she'd read him so easily? "How should I know his methods?" he countered. "The information was accurate. That's all I cared about."

Nikki pondered that, then said, "When's he due to be off-loaded?"

"I have no idea."

"We should go now," Johnny said, not sounding the least bit hurried. He bowed to the Dragon. "Your Chou Hai will be eager to return to you."

The Dragon bowed in return. "Your services aboard my vessel, selfish as they were, are appreciated," he said. "And our Russian shipment will be unimpeded?"

Johnny inclined his head, but it was Nikki the Dragon was watching.

"As soon as you let us go and I code the abort sequence," she retorted. "Or else your boat goes 'boom.'"

The Wo Shing Wo collective scowled. Chan fretted, wringing his hands. The Dragon waved them toward the door with fingers studded with flashing gold, as if her words meant nothing to him, but she noted their trembling.

Nikki walked away with Johnny's broad hand on the small of her back, enveloped by a protective pine forest engulfed in clean and laughing rain.

Chapter 7

"So Diviner travels inside his container." Nikki switched hands on the scrambled phone while she talked to the computerized voice of Delphi. "By the time we got back to the terminal, the container was gone, already off-loaded and moved to who knows where."

She didn't try to keep the bitterness from her voice. She'd had Diviner in her sights—right under her proverbial nose—and let him slip past her.

Slip past her. In a ten-ton container.

"And the Sun Yee On?" Delphi asked.

"Back in full force as we were leaving the port," Nikki reported. "The Wo Shing Wo had shown up and it looked like it was going to be the O.K. Corral all over again."

If Johnny was listening, he showed no sign of it. He was efficiently tossing gear into a leather bag while she talked. His apartment wasn't as bachelor-paddish as she had expected from some kind of cop-warrior, but he had plenty of guy-toys to pack: his semiautomatics, throwing knives, nunchaku. A teddy bear.

Nikki blinked. Teddy bear?

"We need Diviner's equipment," Delphi said. "That satellite signal must be his connection to the outside world."

"He paid for his passage on the SHA ship with some kind of information. Is that his angle?" Nikki guessed.

"Maybe." Delphi slowed, sounding thoughtful. "A good cracker can work from anywhere. He'd have to have an entire network of proxy servers to hide behind and zombie computers he can use to break in to anything."

"If he had all that set up, he'd just need a satellite connection to do it."

"Right."

"Problem is, I didn't see anything on any of those containers that even resembled a dish."

"Maybe he's using a new technology."

"You think he's that advanced?"

"We can't rule out that possibility."

Nikki parted the blinds on the east-facing window. No sign of daylight yet. Her body was wide awake but she could feel the fatigue lingering in her bones. Still, she wouldn't stop.

"I won't quit," Nikki said more to herself than to Delphi.

"His equipment may be more valuable than him," Delphi's flat voice replied. "Bring back what you can, if you can."

Nikki's head came up. *If.* Her brothers had taunted her unmercifully with the word. *If* you have the stomach for it. *If* you can do it. *If* you're smart enough. *If* you're strong enough. *If* you're fast enough.

She'd always proven it to them but they'd never quite accepted it. Even Jaime, Jr., closest to her in age and affection, didn't always believe she could do what she set out to do.

Nikki knew intellectually that wasn't what Delphi meant, but old habits die hard and the anger rising within her was an old friend.

"I'll get this *hijo de puta.* Don't worry."

Delphi clicked off.

Johnny regarded her from the futon where he sat fiddling with one of his guns. "Trouble at home?"

"Just reporting in to my boss." Nikki dropped the phone into her own gear bag. The bustier was starting to pinch.

"I have to get this damned thing off," she muttered and stalked into Johnny's tiny bathroom, where her clothes lay neatly folded on the floor.

Tempted by the shower, she took one, then slid into her comfortable, *demure* workout clothes. Much better. She finger-combed her hair's damp ends and took a deep breath.

"You should calm down," Johnny observed when she emerged. "You'll wear yourself out being tense like that."

"I'm tense for a reason," she retorted. "Where were you when I was standing up to a warlord?"

Johnny chuckled, a deep, rich sound lower than his normal speaking voice as he rose from the futon. "He was no warlord. More an administrator."

"He was ready to kill you and sell me to the highest bidder."

"He was a big fish in a very big pond. He enjoyed the game." Johnny gripped her shoulders from behind and squeezed gently. "As I did."

"Which part?" Her throat, she decided, was still sore from the opium smoke. That was why she sounded so hoarse. "The part where I almost passed out or the part where I lost control of my brain and told a thug I'd blow up his boat?"

"All of it," he murmured near her ear. He squeezed again and released her. "We must leave here. We've been followed." He turned her around and cast a critical eye over her clothing. "You can't wear that. You should change."

"If you're thinking I can pretend to be a tourist, I'm pretty sure my cover's blown."

"Where we are going is not for the mission. You need rest and food and to relax."

Nikki scowled. She knew she needed the food

and rest, but how could she relax? Diviner was stumping around somewhere in the Hong Kong shipping terminal, hiding in one of about fifty thousand metal boxes.

"My contact will help us later today." Johnny opened the closet she was beginning to think of as the Closet of Fashion Horrors. "Here." He started to toss a flimsy pale green something at her but stopped. "Bad color for you. Try these." He flung her a pair of jeans.

She glared at the denim where it lay draped over her arm. "Wouldn't it be easier to go back to my hotel and get my own clothes?"

"Perhaps. But we may need a safe place later, and why waste it when these might fit you?" He threw a royal-blue shirt at her. "Go change. We have to hurry."

Nikki's first impulse was to throw the shirt back in his face, but decided that at twenty-four, she was really too old to get into a pissing contest.

Besides, he was better equipped.

That thought burning in her mind, she quickly shut herself in the bathroom and changed again. The jeans were a half size too small and the shirt was too big this time. A sense memory of Johnny's hands moving over her hips rose, unbidden, in her mind.

Chill, she ordered herself. The guy had cast-off clothes from about twenty different women and hands that roamed almost as much as his eyes. That turnoff seated firmly in her brain, she slid the door open.

"Where are we going?" she asked as she gathered up her gear bag.

"First we lose our tail. Then we go to Kowloon, on the mainland. My grandfather has a dojo there." Johnny paused to study her, then nodded his approval of the clothes he'd given her.

She ignored his gesture—she didn't care whether he approved or not—and slung her bag over her shoulder.

"You still have the semiautomatic?" Johnny asked.

"Within reach."

"Good. We must travel quickly."

Johnny snapped off the lights. He moved silently toward the door, tiger-striped by the city light slanting through the living room's open blinds.

For an instant, she could have sworn protective pine lifted through the air behind him, but decided it must be residue from earlier, a scent-memory caught in her nostrils and throat like a dream half-remembered at dawn.

Nikki woke much, much later than dawn. From the sun's position glimpsed through an open window, it was midmorning. She was lying on her stomach and she could tell she'd rolled over violently while she slept because the T-shirt she was wearing had corkscrewed around her waist.

Why was she at Athena Academy in her old room? she wondered. And why were all these first-year students wearing pastel sweat suits and standing around her bed staring at her?

"Munchkins," Nikki groaned.

Titters followed this remark, titters in the high-pitched voices of little girls. Yep, she was definitely at Athena.

Athena.

Nikki's eyes snapped open. Not Athena. Nowhere close.

She shook her head to clear it of too little sleep and coughed, still tasting opium smoke. A little girl, her hair cut to just below her chin, handed her a teacup and bowed.

Nikki rolled over and stared. Beneath her unzipped sweat jacket, the girl was wearing the flimsy pale green top Johnny had declared wasn't her color. *Not girlfriend castoffs,* Nikki thought, and felt a strange combination of troubled and relieved.

She got one arm and hand out from beneath the thin blanket to take the cup. Paint thinner came immediately to mind at the first whiff, but the liquid was off-white and kind of watery.

"Doh je," she muttered in thanks.

She sipped. Some kind of milk, warmed up and a little nasty. Still, she was thirsty and the next sip kind of grew on her.

While she drank, she counted. Five little girls, all about eleven years old. One bed, narrow but surprisingly soft. One standard-issue ceiling fan, rocking in its frame over her head as it whirred gently. One folding panel behind which she remembered dropping her borrowed clothes. One small chest, beside which sat her gear bag, and which held a Sun Yee On soldier's stolen firearm.

The gun.

She set the teacup on the floor with a clatter. The girls scattered at her sudden movement like a flock of spooked birds. She dug into the gear bag's side pocket. Breathed a sigh. It was still there, untouched. She dumped out the magazine and engaged the safety, then slid the gun beneath the mattress.

If she'd known Johnny's grandfather's house would be swarming with little kids, she'd have dismantled the gun before crashing in the wee hours after an exhausting trip hither and yon through downtown Hong Kong to lose the Wo Shing Wo. On Johnny's sport bike.

She tried not to think too much about that.

One of the girls, a beauty with long hair hanging in a shimmering cascade down her back, plopped down on the foot of the bed and smiled. "Hell-o," she tried.

Nikki couldn't help answering both the word and the smile. "Hello."

More titters. The other girls regrouped and started inching forward.

"How ah you?" the girl continued, pausing only briefly between each word.

"I'm fine. How are you?"

The gaggle giggled. The beauty beamed and bowed a little. "Fine." One of the girls pushed the beauty's shoulder and said something. The beauty frowned and snapped something back.

Then she sighed, struggled, and finally said, "Than koo."

"Thank you, too," Nikki replied with a grin.

For whatever reason she couldn't imagine, Nikki suddenly became more accessible and the other four girls piled onto the bed. One grabbed her hand to study an in-the-line-of-duty scar on her forearm. Another pushed her hands through Nikki's curly and sleep-crunched hair. The others chattered amongst themselves while they poked through her bag.

"Hey!" she said, grabbing for her gear.

One of them laughed and dashed out of the room, holding the bag over her head. The others took off after her, shouting.

"Little brats!" Nikki called after them, then chuckled.

This is what it would have been like to grow up with sisters. Always in your stuff. Not respecting your privacy. Getting in your way. Not letting you sleep.

Nikki smiled to herself. She would have loved it.

Her time at Athena Academy was the closest she'd ever come to having sisters. Her friendship with Jess especially. Nikki didn't regret her brothers. Not Rey, who'd dared her into more feats of stupidity than she cared to remember, nor Rico, who'd convinced her that the ballet lessons wouldn't be *that* bad if they'd improve her balance. And certainly not Jaime, who'd seconded her in every playground fistfight she'd ever gotten into.

But there were times when she'd wanted to stay up late on a Saturday night and have a heart-to-heart with someone who knew what it was like to be, well, a girl. And her own age. To have a sister who'd sprawl on the bed with her and talk about dreams and what she wanted to be when she grew up.

Someone who knew what it was like to have the kinds of feelings and worries and hopes she had. Jess had been that sister for her at Athena. Maybe it was they suspected there was something just a little different about them both. Whatever it was that had drawn them together, the kinship remained strong, as if invisible threads had braided a cord that tied them to each other, no matter how far apart they were.

She wondered where Jess was, and hoped she was okay.

Nikki imagined a sister would look at her the way Jess always had, the way the little girl was looking at her now from where she sat, unmoved, on the bed's edge.

"So you're hanging with me instead of your friends, huh?" Nikki asked her.

The girl smiled. A hint of vanilla soap wafted from her when she fidgeted shyly.

"What's your name?"

"Ming-shu," the girl said, but whether that was her name or Cantonese for, "What the heck are you saying?" Nikki didn't know.

"Well, kiddo," she said, throwing back the covers, "let's get going."

Nikki slipped behind the panel. "I can't stay long," she told the girl as she stuck her foot into the black pants she wore for training. "I've stayed too long as it is. Your brother—I assume Johnny's your brother—has been helping me out, but we gotta get outta here. Fight the bad guys, save the world." Nikki tied the drawstring on the pants. "You don't understand a word I'm saying, do you?"

The girl said something, then stopped. Get on with it, Nikki imagined her saying.

"Okay, here's the deal," she continued aloud and stripped off the oversize T-shirt she'd slept in. "Have you ever really loved a place because it gave you everything you needed? That's my school. It's being threatened. I think." Nikki paused as she wriggled into her sports bra. "It was the first place in the world I felt like I really belonged. That's what you get when you grow up with nothing but brothers. They want you to be a boy, even when you're not."

The girl was silent.

"But I'm not a boy."

She stepped out from behind the panel, still buttoning last night's royal-blue blouse, and came face-to-face with Johnny Zhao, who caught her at the waist and cast an admiring glance at her bare throat, then her collarbone, then lower.

"Yes, I know," Johnny said, his handsome face sliding into a devilish grin. "And I'm very glad."

Chapter 8

"Yeah, it would have been a little embarrassing if you'd been groping a guy last night," Nikki said smoothly and jerked her shirt closed. She sidestepped him and quickly finished buttoning up.

"My tactics against the Wo Shing Wo would have been very different," Johnny admitted. "I would have let him protect himself."

Nikki fetched her phone off the floor where it had fallen when the girls hijacked her bag. "I needed protecting?"

Speaking of pushy men. Cop a feel and tickle her tonsils because he thought she couldn't take care of herself? What a jerk. Dead sexy jerk, dressed all in black as he was, but still a jerk.

Johnny waited until she glared at him to say evenly, "It could easily have gone another way."

She felt a flash of annoyance followed quickly by one of shame. She couldn't fault him for doing what he believed would be best. She was in his territory, among his people. They'd managed to get some of the information that Delphi needed, and had a lead on Diviner. Mission partially accomplished.

Okay, so he'd mugged down on her a bit. They were both adults in a potentially dangerous situation. It couldn't be helped.

And he was scentless. Again.

Emotions were curious things. Ulterior motives— the ones sitting behind lies or exaggerations or jokes or some stories—broadcast a beacon of scent. If someone had something at stake, she could usually pick up on that, too.

Facts, like those dispensed endlessly by Dr. Riggings in her senior year Modern European History class, smelled of exactly nothing.

Johnny was a fact-based kind of guy.

She examined that fact and found herself satisfied. Mostly. He occasionally got on her nerves, but his neutrality could be a benefit. If he walked around smelling like an incense factory she would either be distracted because he found her attractive or nursing a migraine from the overload.

It was much better this way.

"You might be right," she said.

"Good." Johnny's dark eyes sparked with anticipation. "Now you meet my grandfather."

Master Wong teetered on the brink of many things: overhospitality, overpoliteness, poverty. In his sixties, Johnny had told her, and he showed no signs of slowing down.

Nikki thought it wasn't slowing down that was his problem. He moved at a stately pace in all he did, from rustling up a traditional breakfast of congee— rice porridge with mushrooms and green onions thrown in—to rounding up the seven little girls who lived with him to drinking his single cup of soybean milk at the low breakfast table.

Today was Master Wong's fasting day.

"When can we get going?" Nikki asked Johnny when they had finished the congee. Most of the girls had already had their morning meal and were spread out in the adjacent room that served as Master Wong's dojo. Only Mingxia and her younger sister, Yanmei, remained in the kitchen.

"I've got a friend tracking down the container we're looking for," Johnny replied casually, setting Yanmei out of his lap, where she'd sat contentedly through the meal clutching the teddy bear he'd given her. "She'll call me when she knows its location and next destination."

"This man you look for is dangerous?" Master Wong asked.

"Possibly. We think he might be a computer

cracker." Johnny poured a post-breakfast cup of green tea for Nikki and himself.

Master Wong simply nodded. "Money. Power."

"El dinero mueve montañas," Nikki said. "Money moves mountains."

"And yet—" the old man tapped his forehead "—there is no mountain."

Nikki kept her face still. Confucius in the flesh, huh? *There is no spoon,* she thought, remembering *The Matrix.*

"He means that the only mountains that exist are the ones we create," Johnny translated. "The only reason I have a problem is because I want something out there—" and he waved his hand at the world "—to be other than it is."

"So I'm supposed to sit back and watch Diviner do his dirty deeds and not care?" Nikki asked. Screw that.

"Not at all." Master Wong smiled beatifically. "We do the work that lies before us."

"We do what we do because we want to," Johnny continued, "not because we're driven by guilt or a need for validation."

She supposed it made sense, sort of. She could see where Johnny would consider his part of this mission to be just "doing the work before him," which was why he wasn't invested in it—and therefore not spewing a cascade of copper pennies or wet-dog fur in her direction because he was angry or anxious.

And yet he was invested a little. On two occasions he'd felt regret over Regina Woo's death, and once she'd made him angry enough to exude a penny scent. He'd told her it was a matter of honor to continue the mission.

And yet… There was nothing there.

Nothing except those sensual lips and strong jaw, the planes of his face and his broad, capable hands now elbow-deep in dishwater.

Master Wong was worse. From him she sensed nothing at all. Did these guys not have feelings like regular people?

Still, Johnny's gentleness with the girls, his patience in letting them clamber all over him and holding Yanmei through his meal, suggested a deep well of *something* inside him. *Still waters run deep,* she'd heard her mother say. Perhaps Johnny's waters ran so deep they didn't lift their scent to the surface.

That thought tugged at her, but Nikki mentally shrugged and moved on. "When's your friend going to call?"

"Soon. You are too impatient." Johnny stood from the camp stool he'd sat on for breakfast and began clearing away the dishes.

Nikki stared. Forget the still waters. He was a judgmental jerk. "Maybe so, but I don't want to lose this guy."

"We won't lose him."

"I'd love to share your confidence, but the last time I looked, nothing chained him to that container he travels in. He could jettison it at will. Then we'll never find him."

"He'll abandon it only if he knows we know he's traveling in it," Johnny pointed out. "He doesn't, so he won't."

Nikki disliked his logic but had to admit he was probably right. She just wouldn't tell him so because he was already pretty damn arrogant. "You're sure your contact can track him down?"

"Yes."

Johnny had gotten through the dishes at a remarkable rate. Master Wong, Nikki realized with a start, had disappeared. When she listened, she heard his voice coming from the dojo.

"Why does your grandfather have all these kids?" she asked.

"He does what is before him." Johnny wiped his hands dry and came back to the table. He sat and gave Nikki a measuring look. "The West assumes our government's one-child policy is absolute, but that's not true. One child is the ideal, but a family can have two if they're willing to pay a social maintenance fee. Still, in our rural areas, girls are not valued as much as boys."

"These are castoffs from parents who don't want to pay a fine?" Nikki felt her throat tighten.

"Some. Others were left because their parents did not want to suffer the shame of having a second girl."

"Aren't there children's protective services or something to take care of these kids?"

"The orphanages do what they can," he replied. "What they can't do, my grandfather does."

"Before they become slaves," Nikki whispered, thinking of the Chou Hai and his boatload of cargo headed to Russia.

"That's one possible future, yes. Factories or sex. Here, my grandfather sees they are clothed and fed. And educated. When another home becomes available, they go there to be cared for."

"They're adopted?"

Johnny nodded. "My grandfather doesn't like to split siblings, so he still has Mingxia and Yanmei."

Nikki stood, suddenly restless, and paced to the doorway between the living area and the dojo. Light filtered through the open windows that graced the outer wall, spilling in elongated squares over the hardwood floor where the girls had strewn themselves for a drawing lesson. Master Wong stooped next to each one in turn as they carefully dipped slender brushes into ink pots and drew swooping, gorgeous lines on parchment. Mingxia had her hand on her little sister's wrist, guiding her movements as she drew a complex character.

"It's not everything," Johnny said at her shoulder, "but it's what he can do."

She nodded. People like Master Wong existed all over the planet, taking in the lost and abandoned that no one else wanted. Though child-care professionals might complain that one old man caring for seven little girls wasn't the ideal situation, it was more than most people could or would do. People had jobs and children of their own.

But to think of girls as less than. To feel shame over giving birth to a girl rather than a boy. Nikki couldn't imagine it, and, cultural sensitivities aside, she felt a sense of anger on their behalf.

"See!" Yanmei squealed, pelting over to Johnny with her parchment.

He bent and scooped her up, then admired the paper she held up. He spoke to her quickly in Cantonese, then said in English, "What does that say?"

Yanmei smiled at Nikki and tucked her forehead against Johnny's neck.

"Come on," Johnny coaxed. He spoke again in Cantonese.

Yanmei straightened and pointed at the beautiful symbol she and her sister had drawn. "East!"

"Yes. Very good."

"Vah good," she replied.

He said something again in Cantonese, and she responded once more, "Vah good."

"Smart girl." Johnny scuffed her hair and set her down. She ran back into the dojo and plopped down next to Mingxia, ready to draw her next character.

"You're good with her," Nikki observed, recognizing the signs of a man at home with children and ignoring the tug that thought provoked in her chest.

Johnny shrugged. "She's easy to be good with."

"Is your grandfather teaching them English?"

"Yes. It will help in school and getting a job."

A bell sounded, echoed through the dojo. On cue, the little girls gathered their parchments and scurried back into the living area. They dutifully spread the papers on the table to dry, then took themselves off in a flurry of pigtails.

"Where's the fire?" Nikki asked.

"My little ones have their reading," Master Wong said. He stacked the ink pots and brushes near the sink along the wall. "Now, we practice." He bowed slightly to Nikki. "You may join us, if you wish."

Practice was sitting cross-legged on a cushion for a half hour of mindfulness meditation, which Nikki didn't come close to mastering. Trying to become aware of everything going on around her was easy— that was part of what she did in the course of her job. But her job insisted she concentrate on her surroundings for a purpose: spot the hidden threat, catch the drug smuggler, save the boat refugees.

Concentrating on her sensory impressions for the sake of…sensory impressions…was a little unnerving. Thoughts threaded through her mind, sort of like opening Pandora's box, which reminded her of mythology, which brought her back around to Hecate, goddess of the crossroads, except that she wasn't originally Greek, was she? And wasn't she originally goddess of the wilderness and childbirth? And her symbol was the black hound, which when she hit puberty Nikki had found disturbingly apropos in *her* case because that's when her gift had kicked in, the nose and all, and that was the year she'd taken trigonometry with Ms. Wilson, and then— Was that a *mockingbird?* Here in *China?*

By the time she got her mind settled down to listening to the songbird, the bell had sounded again.

Master Wong and Johnny unfurled a wide mat over the scuffed hardwood floor while she climbed onto a wall-hugging stool. Master Wong's voluminous clothing fluttered when he opened another of the dojo's tall windows. Outside, shocks of early summer flowers nodded in a steady breeze, scenting the room.

"Verbena," Nikki said.

Master Wong's entire face seemed to smile. "Yes. Very good."

He motioned her to stay where she was, then slipped into soft shoes and paced to the center of the makeshift ring. After a moment, he bowed low to his grandson.

Johnny stepped onto the mat. He'd stripped to only the black fighting trousers he'd worn the night they'd met—what, like *yesterday?*—and was barefoot. His lean, muscled chest rippled as he stretched his arms back over his head, then behind. When he deemed himself ready, he bowed low to his grandfather.

They began to dance.

Grandfather and grandson moved perfectly to the kung fu form, grandfather taking defensive moves and grandson taking offensive ones. The smooth, circling strikes and kicks were poetry made by the human body, moves of indirection, deflection, turns that directed energy away or back.

Nikki sat mesmerized by the flow, back and forth,

around the mat, the long, looping moves of the two men practicing this ancient martial art. She'd studied Tae Kwon Do in college, appreciating its blunt force and sudden, violent movements, and had done a short stint in hapkido, with its attention to joint locks and breaks.

But kung fu—no, this was *Chon Fa*—took her breath away.

The two men circled the mat again, and this time Nikki noticed Johnny's back. A neat scar, long healed, slashed his skin from shoulder blade to neck. When he turned or lunged, it flexed on his skin like a tattoo over muscle.

Had the cut been deep? she wondered. Had he nearly died? A cut like that could have sliced open a lung.

When she looked more closely, she found other long-healed scars striping his shoulders and upper arms in a tapestry of pain.

Johnny and Master Wong completed their form by bowing to each other. Master Wong waved to her. "Your turn."

"I don't know the art," she protested.

"Come! I will show you," he replied.

Johnny waited impassively, sweat just beginning to dot his firm pecs. "My grandfather's teaching is legendary," he said. "You should listen to him."

Stifling her annoyance at his bossing her around— again—Nikki shed her shoes and stepped onto the mat. Master Wong patiently took her right hand. She automatically formed a fist, but he tapped it.

"Too rigid. Energy must flow."

She relaxed it into a loose fist.

"Good." Master Wong held her new fist up and nodded. "Warrior hand, hand of strife and force." He patted her knuckles. "Bring other hand to knuckles."

She placed her left palm flat against her right fist's knuckles.

"Good. Open hand is the hand of peace, stopping warrior hand. All is balance. Now bow."

Nikki bowed to him.

"Chin up, eyes lowered. Proud but humble."

She bowed again.

"Good. Now, you saw the form." He gestured toward Johnny. "Take your place."

She inwardly grimaced. She'd seen the form exactly once, had only paid partial attention to the moves, and was about to humiliate herself in front of two men for whom "proud but humble" ranked right up there with "handsome but bossy." Nikki sighed.

Johnny waited. She read no expectation in his expression, but then, she read very little from him, anyway.

They bowed to each other. Nikki focused on the hollow of his throat. From there, she could be aware of his arms and legs. And avoid those dark eyes that radiated such frustrating neutrality.

He stepped forward with a knife hand. She countered with the sweeping block Nikki remembered his grandfather using, then executed a front kick.

Johnny's block was featherlight, barely touching her before he advanced with a palm hand.

And suddenly, she was there, in the zone, her eidetic memory calling up the form in detail, her body flowing with the energy that seemed to swirl around and between them as they moved. Even the complicated block-block-strike-parry combination that she'd admired welled up in her muscles and blood. She knew only the sweat glistening on Johnny's golden skin, their feet slapping and squeaking on the mat, the slight touches symbolizing the strikes that could, if thrown in earnest, break bone.

She became aware of Johnny picking up the pace, moving faster with his lunges. Heat radiated from his body as he advanced. She held her ground, moving swiftly, silently, to the side as he pursued her around the mat. Circling once, then twice, until they met in the center in the close-quarters punches and blocks that had them practically in each other's arms.

Sandalwood abruptly overwhelmed her senses. Her mind blanked.

When she looked up from the floor, her jaw ached. Johnny leaned over her, his brow furrowed and wet-dog fur—anxiety—emanating from his heated skin.

"Are you all right?" he asked.

"Is it still Tuesday?"

He grinned and held out his hand. "I went too fast. I'm sorry."

Her jaw hurt, bad. "I thought you were barely touching me."

He shrugged apologetically. "My chi became… aggressive. To match yours." She allowed him to hoist her to her feet, but he didn't step away or let go of her hand. "Forgive me. I forgot myself."

Nikki inhaled deeply. "Next time, *I* go on offsense."

He backed off, grinning, and they bowed.

She hid her smile until she turned away, flooded with the scent of his sandalwood.

Chapter 9

"I have not seen a pupil take such care with her practice," Master Wong told Nikki a few minutes later when he handed her an ice pack for her jaw. "You learn quickly."

Nikki shrugged. "It's just a memory thing."

Master Wong's steady gaze felt as if it was boring through her skin. He gestured for her to sit on a wooden bench arranged beneath a wall of weapons—swords, the staff, throwing stars, *sai,* nunchakus hanging from their chains. "Your skills are more than memory or rote. You are a natural warrior. You anticipate rather than expect."

Nikki pondered that last statement as she watched Johnny teaching Mingxia to strengthen her fighting stance. She *anticipated* a phone call from Johnny's contact at the shipping terminal. She *expected* Johnny to make light of it, as if Diviner would be waiting around indefinitely. It was already getting into late afternoon, and still no phone call from his friend. Nikki blew a sigh.

At Master Wong's querying look, she said, "I'm sorry. I have a lot on my mind."

"My grandson will help you through. He is an honorable man."

Nikki's mind flashed on the hot dance at the Electric Dragon that was supposed to have protected her virtue. "I'm sure he is," she said, knowing she sounded like she didn't believe the venerable old man sitting beside her.

"You remind me of my daughter," he said.

"Johnny's mother?"

He nodded once. "She was quite skilled. Not the natural you are, but had I started her training earlier, perhaps she might have made up in work what she lacked in heart."

Johnny was now facing Mingxia, straightening her shoulders into proper form for the horse stance.

"Her choices might have been wiser. Johnny might not have suffered so much."

"What kind of suffering?"

Master Wong nodded at his grandson. "Johnny's father expected much from his oldest son. More than a child should be asked to bear."

She thought of the scars that laced Johnny's back. "Did he expect Johnny to become a cop?"

"Far from it. My grandson was a great disappointment to him."

Master Wong seemed to settle into stillness and Nikki fell silent. Whatever Johnny's parents had or hadn't done, it sounded pretty serious and Nikki didn't want to set foot in that territory with a man she'd just met. She dropped the ice pack from her face and gingerly pressed her fingertips against the bruised flesh. Tender. She probably looked like she'd been slugged with a baseball bat. That's what it had felt like.

Johnny had barely tapped her.

Yanmei ran into the dojo and leaped onto Master Wong's lap. Nikki wondered if she herself had run everywhere at full tilt when she was seven. Probably. She'd been running away from one brother or another, or playing games with them, or chasing them down. God, she'd grown up such a tomboy.

But where her brothers had teased and challenged her constantly, Johnny guided Mingxia gently, as if he understood the child's diffidence. Nikki swallowed down the lump rising in her throat. He was such a calming presence, getting Yanmei to sit quietly through breakfast, now coaxing Mingxia, who clearly wasn't comfortable in her body yet.

Johnny infuriated Nikki as much as he relaxed her. It was always a toss-up which way it was going to go between them, she thought. One minute they were just sparring and the next someone was getting hurt.

Outside, the wind shifted, bringing the overconfident, triumphant scent of lemons.

"Do you have a lemon tree?" Nikki asked Master Wong.

He shook his head.

"Johnny! Someone's here!"

As if she'd called them, a pile of black-garbed men spilled through the dojo's open windows.

Nikki grabbed Yanmei. "Mingxia!"

The little girl ran toward her. Nikki sent them both into the kitchen. "Run to your room!" she shouted, hoping Mingxia's English was good enough to understand the command.

She turned. Johnny and his grandfather had become leaping, spinning forms amid flashing silver knives.

A dark form barreled toward her, knife at the ready. She yanked the closest weapons at hand from the wall—a pair of *sai*. With a flick of her left wrist, she caught her attacker's knife blade between the long center blade and barb of her trident-like weapon and levered the knife away. She jabbed the *sai* she held in her right hand into his thigh. Snarling, he wrenched himself back.

She let him run. The crack of a gunshot, then another. Holes blossomed in the wall near her head. Master Wong disappeared beneath a pile of bodies. She started forward, then the men sprang back, flung aside as if Master Wong had blown them off with the force of dynamite.

One fell in her direction. She met his incoming

chest with a solid front kick to the sternum. He shrieked and landed on his knees, gasping for air. She popped his skull with a heavy *sai* butt. He went down.

She lost sight of Master Wong. Three men were converging in Johnny's general vicinity, the one behind reaching beneath his shirt. Cursing, she dropped one of her *sai* and snatched a throwing star from the weapons wall. She'd never used one, but she'd played a mean second base.

In a breath, she saw her target clearly as he raised his arm, revolver in hand. Men passed between them, chasing someone. She leaned back, slipped on the hardwood, caught her balance, threw. The star vanished, as if by magic, and reappeared buried to the hilt in the man's bicep.

The gun fired.

"Johnny!" Nikki shouted.

He was rolling on the floor with one of his two remaining attackers, punching as they spun. The other man raised his knife, ready for an opportunity.

Nikki grabbed her dropped *sai* and waded in. Someone clutched her upper arm in a painful vise grip. She reversed her hold on the *sai* she still held and rammed it back toward her attacker. She missed, but he let her go.

She sprinted across the mat toward the knife man and gave him a hearty kick from behind. The groin shot put him down, writhing. Johnny got two good punches in on his attacker. The man's arm flailed as

Johnny pinned him, and without hesitating, Nikki buried the *sai* blade through the man's palm and into the floor. His screams screeched, cutting through the last shouts.

In a sweeping movement, Johnny was on his feet. He trapped another attacker's foot between his hands and gave it a vicious twist. Nikki heard bone snap and the man writhed on the mat.

And then there was nothing but the groans of the downed soldiers—Wo Shing Wo from the Electric Dragon, Nikki assumed.

"Did we get them all?" she asked.

Johnny had already snatched his cell from a shelf and was dialing someone. While she counted the wounded, she could understand suddenly how Johnny had quietly disarmed and disabled ten men within fifteen minutes while staking out a container ship. She'd never seen anyone move with such economy of motion and effort.

Master Wong, she decided, was a Jedi master.

Johnny tossed her a knotted climbing rope while he spoke into the phone. She quickly tied the wounded soldiers' hands behind their backs in a killer set of palomar knots, kicking their weapons out of reach as she went.

"It's bad news when the Wo Shing Wo know where your grandfather lives," she said to Johnny when he hung up.

"These aren't Wo. They're Sun Yee On."

"How can you tell?"

"I've seen some of them—" he glanced at two of the men, who glared death threats at him "—around."

"Ah," Nikki said. Johnny's undercover work had taken him into Sun Yee On territory, then. Nikki checked the pulse of the man she'd pinned to the floor. "What are they doing here?"

Johnny shook his head, and the wet-dog anxiety he carried with him became palpable. "I want to know where my grandfather is."

"I am here," the old man said.

He stood framed in the kitchen doorway, his face grave and lacking the light that had seemed to radiate from within. "Mingxia and Yanmei have been taken."

Nikki felt the world condense to the roaring in her ears. Those precious little girls.

Without thinking, she picked up one of the guns she'd taken and pointed it at the closest thug on the floor. "Where've they taken them?" she shouted.

Johnny murmured in Cantonese to the guy, who spat, "I heard her."

Nikki dropped to her knees and fisted his shirt with her free hand. "Then answer me, damn you."

The Sun Yee On soldier sneered through bleeding lips. "Fuck off, *gwai-poh*." He spat blood in her face.

She leaned back, wiping the coppery spittle from her skin. Then she sighed and looked up at Johnny, whose tense stance suggested he was not as casual about this situation as his face made him appear. "Can I have him?"

"You shouldn't," Johnny warned. "The cops will be here in a few minutes."

"But I want the information." Her words were even, measured. "I want it *now.*"

"It's not wise. I can't let you—"

Nikki turned her body so the Sun Yee On soldier couldn't see her and winked solemnly at Johnny. His lips quirked. Good. He understood what she wanted to do.

She pointed the gun at Johnny's face and spoke, starting off softly but gaining volume with each word. "I said I want it now!"

The soldier on the floor cringed.

Nikki glared at Johnny, who'd raised his hands in surrender. "We can bury his corpse in the courtyard." She gestured at Johnny's grandfather. "Start digging a grave."

Master Wong shuffled toward the kitchen.

"Is this gun even loaded?" Nikki abruptly turned the gun up and ejected the cartridge into her palm.

Johnny warily squatted next to the sweating soldier. "Look, tell me quickly, before she gets really angry. She is not quite—" He motioned to his head. His unspoken implication: crazy American woman.

"Fuck off," the Sun Yee On thug snarled.

Nikki placed her foot on the soldier's knee and leaned. He howled.

"Come on! Don't be stupid! You're Sun Yee On, right?" Johnny asked urgently.

This time the soldier nodded. The black cloth

wrapped around his face slipped. Johnny gently lifted his head and unwound the wrap. "That should help you breathe better, huh?"

The soldier scoffed, apparently affronted by the consideration.

Nikki tucked the gun under her arm, then popped the first bullet out of the cartridge and into her hand. "One," she muttered to herself.

"Give me your street name," Johnny coaxed.

"Tsu-Fan."

"Now, what are you doing here?"

"We were sent," the soldier said.

"Is this neighborhood your territory?"

Another nod.

When he appeared reluctant to say more, Johnny pressed. "You were sent to do what?"

Tsu-Fan grimaced. "We're not on Sun Yee On business."

"Then who are you working for?"

Nikki pretended to ignore the conversation, concentrating instead on her task at hand. Bullet number two popped out and clicked against its mate.

The soldier's voice wavered. "We don't know her name. We were told only a powerful woman wanted a man being held here."

"What man?" Johnny pressed. He kept glancing at Nikki, as if afraid she'd lose patience.

Click.

Tsu-Fan swallowed. "I don't know. We know only that he arrived last night."

"At the port."

"Yes!"

Nikki stayed focused. Click.

Sweat beaded the soldier's face.

"What's the man's name?"

"We weren't told."

"Why do you think he's here?"

The soldier's eyes narrowed. "Isn't he?"

Johnny ignored his interest. "Who was this woman?"

"I tell you I don't know!"

Click.

"Four!" Nikki announced. "But I guess that's enough to do the trick, isn't it?" She aimed the empty gun at the soldier's right hand. "One." His left hand. "Two." His right foot. "Three." His left foot. "Four."

She smiled, then tilted the gun slightly to examine it. "Lucky me! One in the chamber!" She swiftly aimed at the soldier's crotch and he gave a strangled cry.

"Who was she?" Johnny demanded.

"They called her *zhizhu*."

"Spider?" Johnny asked. "You're sure?"

"Yes!"

Spider. Arachne? Nikki tamped down the excitement surging in her chest. She turned away and started reloading the cartridge at the same leisurely pace she'd used to unload it. The first bullet snapped smoothly into the cartridge. Snick.

"Who's your Red Pole?"

The soldier jerked his head toward the man whose hand was still staked to the floor. "He got his orders from the *zhizhu*."

"Going behind his boss's back, huh? Wei won't be happy when he finds out."

"How do you know about Wei?"

Johnny snorted. "Who doesn't know about him?"

Snick.

The soldier's eyes were reddening, and he was starting to look nauseated.

Then Nikki smelled angry wet pennies as Johnny switched gears. "Where were the girls taken?"

Tsu-Fan's shoulders dropped and some of his bitter coffee scent dissipated.

Snick.

"I don't know. Maybe they'll be returned in exchange for the man we came to find."

"The nameless man."

The soldier shrugged.

"And if they're not being held for ransom?"

"They'll be taken to the usual place."

Snick.

"And where's the usual place?"

Nikki slapped the cartridge into the 9 mm, waiting for the soldier's answer though she already knew, with rising rage and sinking heart, where they were headed.

"To the boat, to go to Singapore. Where else?" Tsu-Fan shrugged again. "It's all they're good for."

Nikki spun. In a heartbeat she visualized herself

raising the gun, squeezing the trigger, pumping all five rounds into the Sun Yee On's chest.

But he was already downed, knocked out, and Johnny was shaking out his hand.

Her mind's eye flashed on the girls, terrified, struggling against the black-garbed street thugs carting them off, and she swore violently.

"What?" Johnny asked.

Nikki ran to the bedroom all the girls shared. It sat forlorn, the sleeping pallets tangled and piled in a corner, a potted plant overturned, soil spilling in a wide swath beneath the open window. In the kitchen, she heard the other girls weeping, and Master Wong's comforting voice. At her feet, one of Yanmei's pigtail ribbons lay wrinkled on the floor.

Nikki knelt to pick up the ribbon. She smoothed it on her thigh, then set down the gun to quickly tie the pink ribbon around her wrist.

Now, to work.

In a single, deep breath, Nikki detected vanilla and bitter coffee—Mingxia and her fear—along with a curious scent that reminded her of hot tires.

What the hell was that?

She traced the mingled vanilla, coffee and tires to the window. Outside, clear footprints were stamped into the soft earth and led to a gap in the rickety fencing that demarcated Master Wong's property. Nikki backtracked to the house's front, picking up a curious Johnny as she went. She tracked the fence around to the back and found the gap.

There. Amid the alleyway's rotting fish and old cabbage, the vanilla faded fast. It was merely a physical scent carried on the girls' bodies, so Nikki didn't expect it to last in the assault of other physical odors. But the coffee and tires remained.

"Nikki, we can't leave. My colleagues from the Hong Kong police will be here soon." Johnny caught at her arm.

"I'm tracking them!" She jerked her arm from his grasp.

"You can't do that here," he protested. "Where are the footprints?"

"I don't need footprints or broken twigs or bread crumbs." She took a few steps down the alleyway, lost the coffee, then picked it up again a little to the right.

She tucked the gun she still held into her waist-band, where it would be hidden beneath the blousy tail of her untucked shirt, and broke into a trot.

This section of the Yau Ma Tei neighborhood seemed to be crumbling around them, with narrow streets winding crazily between open-air shops as a brisk breeze cut through the trees, all of which were busily scattering the scents Nikki sought.

She traced back and forth across the paths, darting down a side street only to come back and try another. The tire smell was fading now, overcome by diesel fumes and car exhaust.

Burnt coffee teased her, wafting in and out of her olfactory range, gaining strength then disappearing altogether until Nikki found the right direction and kept going. She lost the scent for several heart-stopping seconds until she crossed into a more affluent part of the neighborhood where the roofs no longer sagged and where the food offered at the open market stalls seemed fresher and more exotic.

She was aware of Johnny following at a distance, as if afraid of disturbing her. She was aware of residents and shopkeepers stopping what they were doing to gawk at her. She was aware of just how ridiculous she looked as she traced the scent back and forth across the pathways and streets, dodging cars and pedestrians as she went.

Then she caught the scent again—stronger now. They were close. She reached for the gun's hilt as she turned the corner…

And found herself in the middle of a broad avenue lined with prosperous shops and well-dressed patrons who sat at open-air cafes and sipped from stylish white espresso cups.

Chapter 10

Nikki fumed as she watched the Hong Kong police hustle the Sun Yee On who could still walk into a dumpy white police van. Police ambulances had already carted off the wounded.

Two hours of interrogation by Johnny's HK buddies from the Organized Crime and Triad Bureau, and the cops still weren't happy with the story she and Johnny were weaving about a raid to kidnap children and sell them on the skin market as prostitutes. The cops weren't happy even though that part was the truth—as much of the truth as she and Johnny had agreed to tell, anyway—and even though they suddenly had a van full of gang members off the street, not to mention the small collection she and

Johnny had delivered from the port to their doorstep the day before.

Inspector Richard Lam just kept looking at her strangely, as he had when Johnny had told him that she was the one who'd impaled the Sun Red Pole with the *sai*. His expression fell somewhere between horror and disbelief, and he kept stealing glances at her, like she was a sideshow attraction.

Guilt gnawed at her stomach. The real sideshow attraction was her nose, and she'd been so intent on harassing the Sun Yee On captive that she'd forgotten to use it to track the girls while they could still be tracked, before their scent wafted away on the evening breeze. Her throat tightened.

If the escaped Sun Yee On planned to use Mingxia and Yanmei as bait, for whatever reason, Nikki would be glad to take it. Anything to get those precious little girls back.

In the meantime, someone else was now apparently looking for Diviner—someone who knew not just his general whereabouts, but that she and Johnny had been looking for him.

On top of that, she was starting to drag. Her body thought it was about three in the morning and was complaining that she should have been asleep *hours* ago. All the excitement and adrenaline hadn't sufficiently reset her timing and she wondered what it would have taken to do that. A bomb going off? Running for her life for twenty-four hours?

God, she was tired. She was getting delirious.

"Nikki!" Johnny waved an imperious hand but she didn't have the energy to even think about getting annoyed. With a sigh, she abandoned her station at the dojo's main entrance where she'd been watching the thugs get loaded up, and crossed the mat to join Johnny and Inspector Lam.

"We might have some information on the triad," Johnny said.

Inspector Lam tore his gaze away from Nikki's hands, which were still caked with dried blood, and nodded. "Last night the Wo boys murdered the Sun Yee On second-in-command."

Johnny's brows quirked up. "How?"

"They found out he was planning to meet a slave dealer up in Shanghai. He never made it to the plane. We pulled his body out of a sewage drain early this morning."

So the Electric Dragon—the Wo Shing Wo second-in-command—had used Diviner's information to track down and kill his Sun Yee On counterpart. "This dead Sun guy had caused the Wo Shing Wo a lot of grief?" Nikki guessed.

Lam's startled look, she decided, must be habitual. "The dead man had organized the last big raids against the Wo that nearly put them out of the opium business."

"Settling an old score," Johnny said softly. He didn't look at Nikki. He didn't have to.

"Sure, the Wo were," Lam agreed. "But there's something new going on. Some factions of the Sun

Yee On have started taking their orders from a so-called Spider Woman."

"Yes, we got that much from the man we questioned. Surprising," Johnny mused.

"Not as surprising as this. The Wo Shing Wo have been hired by *another* woman."

"Hang on," Nikki said. "A couple of well-heeled organized crime operations are hiring themselves out as foot soldiers to two *women?*"

"It's not unheard of," Lam said. "The next lieutenant in line for position of the Sun Yee On Deputy Mountain Master is rumored to be a woman. Besides, if the money is right…"

Of course. *Por dinero baila el perro.* "The dog dances for money," she said aloud.

"Who's this other woman?" Johnny asked.

Lam shook his head dismissively. "They claim it is the great-great-great-granddaughter of Chang Wu Gow."

Johnny snorted.

"What?" Nikki asked. "Who's that?"

"Urban legend," Lam replied.

"Chang was a giant," Johnny explained, "about eight feet tall. He died in England in the late eighteen hundreds. He had two sons, and it's rumored that one of his grandchildren inherited his great height."

"And that his giantess offspring moved back to Hong Kong a few years ago," Lam added. "Nonsense, really."

Johnny crossed his leanly muscled arms over his

chest. He had taken the time to pull on a white T-shirt that stretched taut over his shoulders. "Legends aside, the fact the Spider Woman and her rival do not conceal their gender shows their strength," he observed. "They conceal instead their names, or hide behind symbols."

"Then they have power but no peace," Master Wong said as he joined them. "They are seeking what will never make them content."

"Sir." Inspector Lam bowed respectfully to Master Wong.

"Do you still remember the lessons I taught you?" the old man asked.

"I try, sir."

Master Wong nodded. "Then you will find my children."

Lam nodded, and he and Johnny continued their discussion of likely drop-off points where the girls might have been taken.

The range of scent lifting from Master Wong during the conversation dumbfounded Nikki. From anger to sadness to a fierce protectiveness, all in the space of less than a minute. It was, she recognized, the array of emotions anyone would experience when losing a child. But where someone else might have lingered in the anger, and perhaps, she thought with shame, let that emotion cloud their judgment, it flowed through Master Wong like a river, experienced and then released.

His emotions didn't control him. The flash of

insight was so unexpected—and such flashes were so rare for her—that Nikki knew it must be true.

When Nikki snapped out of her thoughts, Johnny and Inspector Lam looked like they were just this side of a fistfight.

"You must stay here," Inspector Lam insisted.

Johnny leaned forward slightly, arms now uncrossed and his body smelling clearly of wet pennies. "We can help you find the girls!"

"You and your family are implicated in a gang war," Lam continued. "As a courtesy to your grandfather I am not letting my men tear through the place and scare the other children."

Johnny scowled at that. He snorted and stalked to the kitchen, where some of the girls remained congregated, wide-eyed. He tousled the nearest's hair, then motioned them away. They scattered out of sight, presumably back to their shared bedroom.

Nikki wanted to help but had no idea even where to start. It wasn't just the cultural differences that inhabited the abyss between her and these men; it was the unfamiliar police procedures, the obvious personal respect Lam seemed to have for Master Wong, the fact that she wasn't sure what her real status was in this country.

If Johnny was basically placed under house arrest, did that mean her, too? Would they expect her to follow their rules despite suspecting there was something besides kidnapped girls involved?

The other problem, too, was how she was supposed to figure out who these women were. The Spider Woman, whom she suspected might be Arachne, was definitely interested in Diviner, but was it really this giantess who had hired the Wo Shing Wo to guard him at the port? Or had Spider Woman hired the Sun Yee On *after* she found out the Wo Shing Wo had brought Diviner here on their SHA container ship?

As she watched Inspector Lam gather up his men, some in crisp uniforms and some in the traditional rumpled Western-style suits that were apparently the universal uniform of the police detective, she wondered if any of this was part of what Delphi wanted her to check out.

She slipped through the kitchen—Johnny had disappeared—and found her way back to the tiny bedroom she'd slept in. She calculated the time change before using the speed dial number coded into the phone, but then shrugged. She didn't even know for sure if Delphi was located in the United States.

It took only seconds to connect to the computerized voice, provide the appropriate codes and passwords to prove her identity, and then fill in the mysterious speaker—she was almost convinced it was a woman—on the developments.

"I don't think I've been sequestered by the police," Nikki said after giving Delphi as much information as she knew.

"Your priority is Diviner," Delphi said, and Nikki wished she could smell the woman so she could tell if the hesitancy in her tone really was regret. "I'm sorry about the children."

"I understand." Nikki's throat abruptly closed and she set her jaw against a sudden desire to cry.

"The stakes are higher than even those children's lives, Nikki. If this Spider Woman is Arachne, she might be after more than just Diviner. She's after special girls like you. She's already succeeded once."

"Yeah, I know."

"Imagine what she could do with a genetically modified girl or woman. Your gift, modified again and again, could create a superrace of bloodhounds doing her will."

"Chasing down her prey," Nikki said.

"I know it's not fair to ask you to stick to the mission, but I have to. You understand why."

Nikki could only nod. She'd suspected that. She didn't like feeling like a chess piece shoved around on a board not of her own choosing, but that couldn't be helped. Her queen was ultimately the Athena Academy, and if following Delphi's orders kept the academy safe, so be it.

But Mingxia's lovely dark eyes and Yanmei's pig-tailed, running form haunted her. They weren't pieces in this particular chess game, but they'd been pulled onto the board, anyway.

Nikki managed to say, "As soon as the police leave, I'm headed back to the port terminal."

"It might be worth biding your time until Zhao's contact is able to get a lead on the container," Delphi advised. "I know you're eager to get out there, but there are times when patience pays a higher dividend than you might think."

Nikki gritted her teeth, hearing her mother's voice in Delphi's intonation. Annoyed, she snapped, "I wasn't planning on going in unprepared. I'm not an idiot."

Delphi waited, silent.

Shit. Nikki scrubbed her face with her hand and said, "I'm sorry. It's pretty tense around here and I just want to get going on this." Her voice rose in frustration. "I feel like I've been spinning my wheels for hours—"

"I understand." A soft chuckle. "I was much like you at your age."

Nikki was suddenly sure Delphi was a woman. Maybe even an Athena graduate? Is that why Athena seemed to be the common denominator, which Dana had implied?

"I advise you to be patient, as I suggested. I suspect you'll make things happen soon enough."

Nikki sighed heavily. "Did you ever get tired of being twenty-four?"

"Often," Delphi assured her. "But what you're doing now will give you experience to rely on later. Trust me."

And almost against her will, Nikki did. She didn't like waiting. She knew she could be a hothead. She knew she had the impulse to just blast into a situation, guns blazing and nose on high alert—and sometimes that impulse had served her well—but maybe this time she needed to do things differently. Maybe Delphi was right.

"I'll try to pretend I'm not Cuban," she muttered.

"Your passion makes you the right woman for the job," Delphi said. "Call me again when you have something new."

Nikki stowed the phone in her belt holster. Yanmei's pink ribbon snugged her wrist. She needed a good cry. She knew it, and she hated it, and she didn't have time for it.

"We'll get them back."

Johnny's deep voice made Nikki raise her head—when had she dropped it into her hands? He stood in the doorway, lean and competent and humming with energy.

Her throat worked for a minute, but she managed to say, "They're telling me to get Diviner. The girls are expendable." It wasn't quite true, but it wasn't quite a lie, either.

Johnny silently came to sit next to her, slipped his arm around her shoulder. Nikki leaned into his anchoring strength, grateful that he didn't speak. Tears pricked her eyes and she let them well and spill. He pressed his cheek to her hair.

She caught old tires again. Part of her wanted to ask him what he was feeling, so she'd know what she was smelling, but part of her didn't care. If Johnny felt it, it was akin to whatever the girls had been feeling.

Then she realized the scent was emanating from her, and that what she was feeling was despair.

Chapter 11

Nikki took one look at Li Bai and didn't like her. She didn't like her long, silky hair that fell in a shimmering raven-fall down her back, she didn't like her long-limbed gracefulness as she sat at her neatly kept desk and she didn't like the movie-perfect makeup that made the woman look like she wasn't wearing any. Nikki didn't like her almond-shaped eyes, her full, richly glossed lips, or her pushed-up cleavage straining her low-cut blouse.

She really didn't like the way Johnny was leaning over the woman's desk, clearly trying to see down the blouse, and the way Bai was angling her shoulders to let him look.

Pretty damned offensive, really, Nikki thought. Impolite. Time-wasting.

She thought harder. *Juvenile.*

She concentrated instead on the view out of the twenty-fourth-story office of the Information and Public Relations Section of the Hong Kong Marine Department. Victoria Harbor spread out below them; bright white ferries and garishly painted private taxi boats coasted through water the color of new denim. In the distance, a container ship appeared to stand still, but its wake lingered like a jet trail on the harbor's surface.

"Did you find what we've been looking for?" Johnny asked, and if voices could drip with anything, his was slathered in raw sensuality.

Nikki tried not to roll her eyes like an exasperated teenager. Bai was the closest thing they had to someone who could figure out where Diviner was going to be loaded up next, and they were at her mercy.

Bai smiled prettily. "I might have it."

"Show me."

The woman turned her flat-panel computer monitor around so Johnny could focus on something other than her chest.

"I'm no longer in the shipping department, so it took me a while to get access to the right database." She batted her long lashes in apparent apology. "Once I got in, I ran several searches. The container was not included in any manifests, so it took some time to find." She cast another sexy smile Johnny's way.

"It was on the manifest in Florida," Nikki pointed out.

"The paper manifest, as you told me, yes, but not the electronic one," Bai said reasonably. "Our database queries aren't set up to find containers that *haven't* been logged," Bai continued in a less flirtatious voice, "so I had to write one that would retrieve containers being loaded onto other ships that didn't have a matching incoming log entry."

Johnny smiled warmly. "Nice."

"It should have been easy, but it wasn't. I had to call in a favor or two to be allowed to write a custom query." Bai flicked a glance Nikki's way. "I'm in marketing communications now. My permissions are quite low on this system."

Clever, Nikki grudgingly admitted as she nodded her understanding. That wasn't something the average marketing suit would know how to do, but this woman had pulled it off.

"I finally found some containers that matched our criteria. Three of them were keyed into the system incorrectly, so that took some time to resolve. We had to track them down manually. The fourth looks like the container you want."

She pointed at an entry on-screen. "The container was transferred here, you see, from Terminal Eight East."

"Where's it going?" Johnny asked.

"Went." Bai did look genuinely apologetic now. "It was scheduled to be loaded two hours ago."

"Dammit!" Nikki muttered. "Where?"

"On a freighter headed for Singapore."

Nikki paced to a worktable holding up a forest's worth of glossy posters and brochures of smiling people in hard hats standing in front of massive, brightly painted cranes and a pristine cargo ship. "So we could have stayed in the terminal and kept watch over the container."

"We still wouldn't know which container we wanted," Johnny said.

The urge to blame, to be pissed off, swept over her. If she'd been smarter, if she'd been more careful, if she'd kept control of the situation instead of handing that over to Johnny Zhao—

"Nikki." His voice was soft now but his hands lay firm on her shoulders. He leaned close to whisper, "We'll find Diviner. It's not your fault."

She shrugged him off and turned to Bai to snap, "Did the container have any identifying marks? How will we know it when we see it?"

"It has four red slashes, like a cat's claws striking," she replied. "The serial number is painted on the side." Bai handed over a sheet with the serial number, freighter registration number, destination and estimated arrival time in Singapore. "I hope you find what you're looking for."

Nikki's nod was terse.

As she strode out to the elevator bank, she heard Johnny murmur something and Bai's low voice replied, with a wealth of undercurrent, "My pleasure."

Nikki let the door close behind her. She wasn't in any mood to put up with their flirtation. Diviner's next destination was in her grasp and she didn't intend to let the *bastardo* get away from her again.

The door abruptly opened and Johnny emerged smelling like a copper mine.

"What the hell was that?" he snapped.

"We got what we came for. Let's get on with it."

"You were rude to my friend."

"Look, you want to flirt with a girlfriend for a couple of hours, great, but you were wasting my time." She punched the elevator's down button. "I have work to do."

"I'm involved in that work. You think I would dishonor Regina's memory?"

She hesitated. "Of course not."

He didn't wait for her when the elevator doors opened, but stalked in. Nikki paused, considering whether to wait for the next elevator, but he grabbed her arm and hauled her into the car with him. "So what's your problem?"

"I should have known about Diviner. I should have figured it out."

"Nobody could have figured it out."

"If we'd had the information sooner, we could have caught the guy here in Hong Kong," she retorted. "Now we have to go to Singapore."

"Bai is trustworthy. Someone else in shipping could have been on the take. I couldn't risk that." He gestured at the paper she held in a trembling hand. "And she got you that."

"Yeah, a day late and a dollar short."

"What?" He frowned in confusion, then dismissively shook his head. He widened his stance as the elevator began to plummet. "You should be more grateful."

"You think I should be grateful that I was hanging out with you while Diviner was getting loaded up on his next ride?"

He grabbed a corner of the paper she held and shook it. "We have this at least."

"It's not enough—"

"It's what we have. This is how things are. You should work with that."

"I'm just saying that it's going to be a lot harder now. *You're* not even supposed to leave Hong Kong."

"That won't be a problem."

"Inspector Lam might be watching you," she pointed out. "Plus we have two street gangs out to get us over this thing and we don't even know what Diviner actually has yet. Everything we know is pure conjecture."

"It'll be fine."

"You can't guarantee that! You're not God, no matter who your grandfather is."

Johnny's jaw clenched hard before he said, "Stop judging me and everyone else because you're not getting your way. This is reality."

"I'm stating the facts as we know them."

"As *you* know them. This is my country, my people. I know who to trust and who to run from. You should listen to me and trust my judgment."

Nikki's throat began to ache. She waited until the elevator slid smoothly to a stop to say, "I'm an adult. I don't need your advice."

"I will give you advice when I see you need it."

Johnny shoved past her as the steel doors whispered open, his anger still filling her nostrils. Nikki watched his back, clad in that gleaming white T-shirt, move away to the tall glass-and-chrome of the foyer. She took a slow step out of the elevator and stopped. Still, he kept walking. She kept standing.

When he reached the revolving door, he almost entered it, then discovered she wasn't there and paused. He said nothing, but waited.

It seemed to her now that something important was happening, that what she was experiencing at this moment was somehow larger than just for this day and this mission. She was watching a strong man, an annoying and strong man, who expected her to cross the wide expanse of marble toward him like a good dog come to heel. Because he insisted on seeing her as *less than*.

She'd not known anyone like him before. Maybe it was that most of the men in her life were her relatives or respected her more or were more mature or maybe it was just sheer dumb luck, but she'd never run into a man who wouldn't even make an attempt to understand her. It was like he hadn't *heard* her at all. Sure, he was a good guy at heart, but there were certain things that no amount of goodness could overcome, and bullheaded arrogance was one of them.

If she walked across that cold, pale blue marble, she'd be giving in, knuckling under, taking on the role he thought she already inhabited.

She couldn't do that.

For an instant, he seemed poised on the edge of walking away, even without her and the information Bai had written on the paper crumpled in her fist. *Go ahead,* she dared him. *See if I care.*

But even as she recognized the childish impulse, he turned suddenly and strode back to the foyer's center. Across the crisp, cool expanse and amid the well-dressed people crisscrossing the space, she felt for a moment as if she'd been immersed in an abandoned but well-stocked library.

Her feet moved since her brain seemed not to be engaged, and she found herself standing with him. The regret she sensed had darkened Johnny's expression.

"We want the same thing," he said. "We should not argue."

More orders, she thought, but decided to accept whatever olive branch he was extending. She simply nodded. He was right—arguing was distracting her from her purpose. They were both losing focus.

It was stupid, really, she mused as she pushed through the revolving door. Getting bent out of shape because of what he thought about her wasn't helping,

either. This trip wasn't personal. It was about Athena
Academy, which was as personal as it ought to get.
   And no more.

Chapter 12

"Our flight to Singapore will leave at seven in the morning," Johnny said as he flipped his cell shut.

Nikki nodded. She knew that. He'd made the arrangements in English. For her sake? she wondered. So she wouldn't feel so…alien?

She sat cross-legged on the floor of his tiny Hong Kong flat, staring at a pile of clothing an elderly woman, with much finger-waving and craning of her bent neck, had just dropped off. Johnny had smiled and charmed the old lady until she left. Now Nikki was folding the hand-me-downs into neat piles. Her own clothes, retrieved from the hotel room she'd barely seen, lay in her gear bag, packed and ready for anything. Except this.

"Great," she muttered. "Another wait."

"We don't have to waste time."

She eyed him warily. "By doing what?"

"Finding out which boat is taking Mingxia and Yanmei."

Nikki's hands clenched in the shirt she was holding. "Talk to me. Where do we start?"

"The Sun Yee On work their child prostitution business out of a warehouse near the port."

She stared at him. "You know that and haven't arrested them?"

"Knowing the facts and bringing a triad to justice are two different things," he said gravely. "In the late eighties, the Sun Yee On Dragon Head—the 'big cheese' you called him—was arrested. The police found a list of nine hundred names that were the Assistant Mountain Master, deputies and Red Poles."

"Nice haul." She reached for a pair of jeans.

"The Dragon Head was convicted based on eyewitness testimony, but was released from prison after only two years."

"What?"

"His appeal went to a judge called Sir Ti-liang. He'd been knighted by the English queen, and was tough enough that his court was nicknamed the Court of No Appeal."

Nikki could see this one coming a mile away. "But he let the Dragon Head off. Insufficient evidence?"

"Almost. A reversal of his previous opinions about allowable evidence."

Nikki laid the jeans in a new pile, then grabbed another shirt. "I hope he was well paid."

"He was. He renounced his knighthood and was given a seat in the Hong Kong cabinet." Johnny's half grin looked more like a grimace. "So you can see that being a police officer can feel…pointless."

Nikki thought that was a bit harsh, but then, for the most part, she saw justice done as part of her work. Drug smugglers thrown in jail or deported, the occasional murderer she came across serving a life sentence. How many criminals—triad members— had Johnny seen walk free?

"Is that why you're not working undercover right now?" She stopped folding to study the broad planes of his face, the hollow look in his deep brown eyes. "Because it's pointless?"

Johnny glanced away. "The OCTB does what it can."

"It sounds like the bureau's hands are tied."

"From within as well as without."

Nikki let that sink in for a moment. "It's corrupt?"

"Not all of it."

"Just the parts that matter."

He didn't have to say anything to that.

So the Organized Crime and Triad Bureau was a *buey*—a castrated bull. No wonder Johnny had seemed weary about stemming the triads' influence and businesses. A thought occurred to her.

"Is Inspector Lam on our side?"

"He upholds the law, yes."

But the faint odor of scorched sheets told her Johnny derided the inspector. "But what?" she asked. "What's wrong with him?"

Johnny frowned at her. "Nothing."

"Look, I know you're not telling me everything. He upholds the law but what? He's weak? He plays both sides?"

"He follows the law," Johnny repeated stubbornly.

"I bet he's ineffectual." When Johnny's deep brown eyes snapped to hers, she knew she was right. "And you're not working undercover because…"

"I bent a rule to arrest a Red Pole. Nothing serious, but Lam let the Red Pole go. He didn't think the charges would stand up in court."

Talk about having your hands tied. Nikki nodded. "I can understand that. Why you bent the rule, I mean. So you've been suspended?"

"For two weeks." He shrugged. "I'm used to it."

"Okay, now that I know the lay of things, what do we do about Mingxia and Yanmei?"

Johnny pulled a map of the Kwai Chung Container Terminal out of the desk wedged in the room's corner, then spread it out on the low-slung coffee table next to where she sat. "The warehouse sits here." He pointed to the northeast edge of the terminal. "They load up passengers in midday, but we think they use the warehouse as a staging area."

"You think the girls are there?"

"Probably, waiting for tomorrow."

Her fingers worried the pink ribbon she wore

around her left wrist. "The Sun Yee On are that methodical?"

"They run a business. They have a regular schedule."

Nikki ignored the shudder that twitched her spine. "What kind of boat do they use?"

"An offshore fishing boat sometimes. Sometimes a ferry."

"That won't get them far, will it?"

Johnny shook his head. "They're usually taken to another staging area, away from the city. Then they're loaded up on a larger vessel for their final destination."

Yanmei's perky pigtails flashed in Nikki's mind. Goddamn slavers. She irritably slapped the folded shirt she held onto a leaning stack.

"We'll get the girls back," Johnny said. "If not tonight, then another time."

"Are we still being followed?"

"Yes, but we can lose them."

She popped an oversize T-shirt out like a sheet. Its mustiness filled her throat and she had to concentrate not to let the scent fill her head as well.

"What are you doing when you do that?" he asked.

"Snapping the wrinkles out."

"No, not that. Frown. Like you're thinking very hard about something very unpleasant." He reached into the clothing pile and pulled out a pair of jeans. "You do it a lot. It's pretty intense."

Your face will stay that way. Nikki intentionally relaxed her forehead. "We should get to the terminal."

"Give me five minutes and talk to me."

One look at his face told her he wasn't going to budge until he had an answer. "I have a physical condition. The concentration helps me control it."

Johnny stared at her for a long moment. "Are you talking about your nose? Your sense of smell?"

She nodded.

"Why didn't you just say that?"

"Because it's *my* business."

"It became *my* business at the club. And a few moments ago when you knew how I felt about Lam."

Nikki suppressed a sigh and couldn't believe what she was about to say. Then she said it. "You're right."

He merely waited.

"It's a long story I don't want to go into, but the bottom line is…" Nikki stopped pretending to fold the T-shirt she held and looked Johnny in the eye. "I have a gift. Sort of. It's hard to explain, but I can tell what people feel from the odors they give off."

Johnny's expression didn't change. Nor did his scent. "You explained that very well."

"Thanks."

He took the T-shirt she held and spread it on the floor facedown. Then in three quick movements he folded it with almost military precision.

"Did you work in retail?" she asked.

He ignored her question. "How does your nose work?"

"It's this hypersensitive thing. I get a whiff of something like coffee, and that translates into fear. Rotting fruit is usually resignation. That kind of thing."

"A smell for every emotion?"

"As far as I know."

"So you know how I feel right now."

"Not exactly—"

"But you said that you can tell what people feel."

"Most people, yeah."

"Then what am I feeling?"

"Right now I don't know."

"I'm feeling something, so what is it?"

"I'm not a performing dog."

"But if you can smell it—"

"I don't know!" Nikki stood and paced to the window. The lights of Hong Kong glared in her face like so many interrogation lights. "Stop being melodramatic," she told herself under her breath. She turned and leaned her butt on the narrow sill, faced his unwavering dark eyes. "You don't give off much of a scent," she admitted. "A whiff here and there."

"Of what?"

"Not much of anything. And very rarely."

"It doesn't seem much good then."

"It's just you," she said. "I spotted the Sun Yee On warriors before they showed up." She thought back for a moment and added, "Your grandfather's worse than you. I can barely read him at all."

"I see."

"I doubt it," she retorted. How could he possibly *see?* "It's annoying as hell."

"Especially if your gift is unpredictable."

"It's not unpredictable."

"What about when you were tracking Mingxia and Yanmei?"

"That's different. I got confused by the physical smell of coffee."

"It's still an error."

Nikki folded her arms over her chest. "What do you want? For me to say my gift isn't worth using?"

Johnny stood and came to her, put his hands on her shoulders. "I'm trying to understand its limitations. If we know where it goes wrong, we can use it more effectively. That's all I mean. Do you understand?"

Under his gently kneading fingers, Nikki felt her shoulders relax, dammit. His touch was too calming, too…peaceful. She wanted to shrug him off but there was no backing away; her butt was firmly planted on the sill. His face had smoothed away its frown, so she was left with his sharp brows poised over large, dark eyes, and a broad nose that looked somehow regal in its flare. And sensual lips that had quirked up into a mischievous smile. His spicy scent of soap and skin filled her mind. Every cell in her body suddenly electrified.

He leaned close to say, "You are not very patient, are you?"

Her throat felt a little tight from the caress his thumbs were giving her neck, so she just shook her head. That movement seemed to draw him closer until his thigh brushed hers. She forgot to breathe.

"Then we should get going." He abruptly released her.

Nikki's next breath hit her hard, because there was nothing—simply nothing—to suggest Johnny had felt anything at all.

Chapter 13

The container terminal sprawled over a good chunk of the northern Victoria Harbor shoreline, and every inch of it was crawling with armed guards.

Nikki, crouched beside Johnny in the Sun Yee On warehouse's shadows, touched the little SW-99 he'd given her. Tucked in a spare shoulder holster, it snugged her rib cage. Nice feeling in a bad place.

The ass-end of the warehouse ran just inside the ten-foot-tall chain-link fence they'd cut into between guard patrols. The warehouse's interior sounded like a construction zone. Hammering, banging and heavy machinery vibrated the metal wall Nikki leaned one palm against. The metal was still warm from the daytime heat. The temperature had dropped enough that she was glad she'd worn a lightweight long-sleeved black top.

"Wait here," Johnny mouthed in her ear.

Before she could argue, he was gone, moving through shadows with feline grace. He slipped between the warehouse and the fence and disappeared. How he managed to walk silently in motorcycle boots, she had no idea.

And if slinking away without her got to be a habit of his, she was going to end up pissed.

It's his town, she reminded herself irritably. Yes, he knew what he was doing and how to do it. Yes, she was a newbie to all this cloak-and-dagger stuff. Hell, the only thing she knew for certain was how sweet the Smith & Wesson 9 mm felt in her hand.

But she still didn't like being left.

She kind of needed him.

She slipped to the warehouse's back corner and looked down its long side. The warehouse's front faced an empty expanse of concrete. Another fifty yards beyond that, containers sat in orderly rows, stacked three high. Into the emptiness, three guards walked casually, rifles slung over their shoulders and gleaming in the light cast down from lamps mounted on the building's eaves. Just as she was thinking about creeping up to the front for a look, the three turned and headed back across the lot.

Fifteen minutes later, the same guards were still pacing, sometimes in a group, sometimes separately. The front entrance was out of the question.

She smelled Johnny, his own spicy scent of soap and skin and something else she couldn't name, before she saw him. Then a tap on her elbow and he whispered, "Come with me."

"What is it?"

"The room where we think they keep the children is inside. Too many guards to get to it from the bay doors or windows. But there's a ventilation shaft from outside. I think it runs over the top of the room where the girls are."

"How far into the warehouse? The room's how far?"

"About a hundred feet."

Nikki suppressed a curse. No matter where she went, she ended up crawling around in the muck and nastiness, rat droppings and dead cockroaches. And worse.

She hated doing that.

"Show me," she said.

He led the way deep into the shadows behind the building, crouching low. Good thing he wasn't a big guy; there was barely room between the building and the fence to accommodate his shoulders. Nikki concentrated on not grinding broken glass beneath her soft shoes, her senses hyperaware of the guards, of their flashlights arcing through the dark, of the scent of machine oil and hot metal and diesel.

"What do they do here?" she asked.

"Fuel tank repair."

She caught a whiff of ginger and raised her hand, silencing his next words.

Not twenty feet away on the fence's other side, a patrol wandered across the parking lot. She and Johnny, hunkered down in the tall weeds lining the fence, froze. Low voices, a laugh, the glint of light on a revolver.

"I thought you couldn't carry a gun in Hong Kong," she whispered when the patrol had passed.

"You can't."

But of course, the bad guys did, especially when they were in bed with law enforcement. Heck, she couldn't legally carry one, either.

Johnny pulled a wicked knife from his boot.

Nikki looked at the vent cover—the tiny vent cover—poised just over her head. "You're kidding."

He grinned, then got to work unscrewing the fasteners that held the cover. "I'm not worried. You can do this."

She doubted it. There was no way she could get her shoulders, much less her hips, through an opening that small. She was still debating how to say no when he popped the cover off.

"Up you go."

"Flashlight first."

Johnny plucked a penlight from his belt and laid it inside the shaft. "Only if you really need it," he warned. "They might see it inside."

"Right."

He cupped his hands. Ignoring memories of those Athena Academy horses—smelly brutes, every one of them—she shoved her foot into his makeshift stirrup and reached for the ventilation shaft. When they both straightened, she got her head into the opening.

She took a long, slow sniff. No rats. No rat droppings. No dead cockroaches. Just a light steam of oil and metal, like you'd expect in a ventilation shaft. She started to feel hope for the first time since they'd arrived.

The sharp aluminum edge nipped at her hands as she levered her head inside. The shaft was surprisingly large, considering. She shoved the penlight forward to give herself room to clamber in. One shoulder wedged in. Her feet started to wander and she resisted the urge to shout at Johnny to hold still.

Then he was shoving hard.

"What the hell?" she stage-whispered, with no hope he could hear her.

"Guards!"

Her internal clock had said they had another ten minutes before the next patrol, dammit. She anchored her elbows as best she could on the floor and dragged herself forward. Her head banged the ceiling. The shaft's opening bit into her hip bones. She stifled a cry. Another hoist, and she'd moved forward enough to get her thighs in. She tried crawling, but her knee struck the shaft side, setting off an echoing *pong*.

Shit.

She felt Johnny's hands on her feet shove hard one last time, and then nothing. She drew her legs up as far as she could. With any luck, the guards wouldn't be able to tell the difference between a covered ventilation shaft and an uncovered one.

With any luck, Johnny would be lying flat on the ground, looking like a discarded pile of overalls.

She couldn't hear anything outside anymore. All that filled her ears was her own breathing echoed back to her, shushing against the aluminum, rasping in her throat. She wiggled. Close quarters. When she'd fleetingly thought the shaft was wider than this, she must have lost her mind.

Her left breast found the penlight boring painfully toward her rib cage. It, plus the shoulder holster she'd neglected to strip off, made the squeeze tighter. She worked the penlight out and held it between her teeth. The holster she'd just have to live with. There was no way she could take it off in here.

Using her elbows, she methodically inched into the warehouse's depths. Pausing every foot to feel the walls, she made good progress. The air oozing toward her, noxious as it was, told her she wasn't headed toward a dead end. The aluminum creaked ominously and she wondered how long it would bear her weight, how long her movements would go unnoticed or ignored.

Her neck started to ache. She couldn't raise her head; it'd bump the top again and alert the Sun soldiers inside to her presence. The sides brushed her shoulders, and if she bent her back just right, she could wedge herself, hips and knees, against the top and bottom. As she eased forward, the shaft seemed to narrow, barely giving her room to do what little shifting and crabbing she needed to move.

Her mind flashed on a news report she'd heard just before boarding her flight to Hong Kong—high school cafeteria workers got to work early in the morning and smelled a dead cat in the walls, but it turned out to be a thief trapped in a vent. He'd been there for days.

She stopped, closed her eyes, and tried to breathe. Burnt coffee surrounded her.

After all the boat holds she'd climbed through, she chastised herself.

Yes, but you had your friends with you.

Johnny's just outside.

Are you sure?

He knows I'm here, she thought, but less certain.

What if he gets killed? No one will know if you get stuck.

Nikki's heart suddenly thundered. The shaft pressed on her skin. Her teeth tightened on the metal penlight. Her eardrums hammered with her pulse.

This is what it was like for Jess, she thought, and remembered the Arizona sunlight shining on her best friend's gorgeous black hair as Jess hooked up her rappelling gear. Nikki had told Jess that a schoolmate was lost, fallen, crying at the bottom of an abandoned silver mine shaft. The scent of bitter coffee had burned in Nikki's nostrils and she'd lain retching in the sand and scrub.

Jess had simply said, "I believe in you," and

dropped into the terrible, horrifying abyss Nikki had been too afraid to enter.

Nikki heard Jess's voice now, echoing back to her over the years and miles as if the words had just been spoken.

Nikki never knew what demons, if any, might have haunted her best friend at the moment she descended. There'd just been that calm acceptance of Nikki's words—her gift—and the decision to risk her life for them.

And less than an hour later, Jess had brought the girl, injured and dehydrated, out of the mine.

The girls. Mingxia and Yanmei.

As she lay flat, her face turned to the wall, Nikki slowly came to realize that her heart was beating more normally. Her breath no longer dragged at her throat like a desperate swimmer. Arms, legs, shoulders, neck: all relaxed.

Thank you, Jess, wherever you are. Stay safe.

Nikki reached forward, testing the walls and floor. Given the work done in this warehouse, it stood to reason that the ventilation system would connect all of the various areas of the building. Even an interior storeroom, where dangerous men might keep child slaves.

And if she could wriggle through the venting system, so could a ten-year-old and her little sister.

Nikki's right hand abruptly went *down*. She slinked forward. Slightly fresher air brushed her cheek. The penlight clapped against her teeth, then she had it in her fist. Covering the penlight's face with her free hand, she flicked the switch.

Her shading hand glowed red and thin streams of light escaped through her fingers. The vent shaft angled straight down, into the ceiling of a room below.

At least twelve feet beneath her, a bundle of old blankets lay rolled up on the floor. A tuft of black hair peeped out. No sound. No movement.

Nikki sniffed.

The burnt coffee still surrounded her, but was it the remnants of her own fear, or the echo of the girls'?

A bang below, and light crashed into the darkness. Nikki flicked off the flashlight. A man's voice barked orders. The bundle shifted, and two, no, three little girls tumbled out of the ratty blankets. From the sounds of the crying that suddenly started, there were more. Maybe six or seven.

Nikki reached for the Smith & Wesson, twisted, tried not to bang the aluminum walls with her knees and elbows. By the time she'd contorted herself enough to draw it, the room was nearly empty. She couldn't drop headfirst, and getting situated for a feet-first jump would waste precious time.

Outside, shots fired.

Johnny!

Had he seen the girls? Had he been seen?

Nikki clamped the penlight between her teeth. She shimmied backward a few inches, then paused when the vent creaked loud enough to be heard over the humming machinery at the warehouse's far end. The voices came back into the room below her, sounding anxious, excited.

Screw it.

She hightailed it backward in a crashing rush, ignoring the pain in her knees and the banging of her elbows. Her heart pounded and her breath became short, sporadic, gasping. When her knees pounded the aluminum, the pong was so deafening it nearly brought tears to her eyes.

Then her feet fell into air and she didn't care whether Johnny was still around to catch her or not—she needed out, now, to get her breath even if it was her last.

Strong hands grabbed her calves, then guided her thighs, caught her butt. She hit the ground hard, then scrambled to get up, pebbles grinding into her palms. Suddenly she had an iron band of a forearm around her waist and her back crushed to a hard chest where a gun butt gouged her.

"Be quiet," Johnny said gruffly into her hair. "You sound like an elephant."

"They were shooting!" she whispered back.

"At you?"

"They had some girls there."

"Ours?"

"I couldn't tell. Does it matter? Who are they shooting at out here?"

"I don't know. Be still."

Nikki leaned against him and tried to breathe. Cars roared to life from somewhere in front of the warehouse. Men, with guns drawn, ran past the shadows where Nikki and Johnny stood riveted together in a patch of shadow. Tires screamed as two Mercedeses made the corner and sped out the fence gate and through the parking lot.

"They're all gathering to the northwest," Johnny said as he released her. "It's probably why you're still alive."

"They were taking the girls out."

Cursing under his breath, Johnny pulled his gun from his shoulder holster. "Where were they headed?"

"I wasn't watching the door and they didn't throw that information out there for me in English, either."

"Shit."

"Come on."

Nikki crept swiftly down the warehouse's side shadows toward its forward bay doors. The fighting had circled out into the containers. Bullets pinged metal, ricocheted from concrete.

In the distance, Nikki recognized the deep rumble of a boat's diesel engines.

"Oh, no. No."

She ducked from shadow to fuel tank to barrel, weaving her way toward the sound of the boat. Each time she paused, she took precious seconds to smell the air.

Vanilla.

Mingxia. And if there was Mingxia, there was Yanmei.

Nikki broke from cover in a sprint. Shouts carried

deep in the forest of containers; the Sun Yee On were still preoccupied.

She made for a small industrial crane standing awkwardly, like a one-legged heron, at the concrete bulkhead fronting the water. In seconds, she had flattened against its steel frame, unseen. Down the shoreline another hundred yards bobbed a huge speedboat, sleek and gleaming in a red-and-yellow flame pattern under the port's lights. Two men were handing cargo down to other men in the boat. Three men stood guard, rifles ready in case the skirmish wandered too close.

A child in a green, filmy top squirmed in her captor's arms.

Nikki reached for the 9 mm. Her hand flailed at the empty holster for a second before she realized she didn't have the gun. Where had she lost it?

Forget the gun.

When Nikki started forward, Johnny's arm caught her around the waist again.

"Don't."

"It's Mingxia!"

"They'll kill you. You won't have a chance."

She knew he was right. Even if they *could* charge in, guns blazing, she and Johnny would be running headlong to their deaths.

Still, she allowed herself the luxury of anger as the men on shore tossed the boat's lines from the cleats. Johnny withdrew, pulling Nikki back with him to the safety of the crane's immense shadows. The Sun Yee

On soldiers turned and loped toward the action, whatever it was, faces alive and alight with eagerness for the fight.

When they'd passed, Nikki tugged herself from Johnny's embrace to watch the wake left by the hell-painted speedboat carrying the girls—and her heart—far out of reach.

Chapter 14

Nikki, one arm clamped around Johnny's waist, wished he'd drive faster. Not because they were pursuing the boat taking Mingxia and Yanmei away—that was impossible—but because she wanted to be away from the busyness and throngs and crush of the city.

The Ducati sport bike hummed along the wide, clean highway that led from Kowloon into a tunnel beneath Victoria Harbor. When they'd snuck back through the parking lot at the terminal and climbed aboard Johnny's bike, he hadn't had to tell her they weren't going back to his flat. She could smell his anger in a flashflood of wet pennies, and she knew from his shadowed face that he needed space and silence. Like she did.

She placed her palm flat against Johnny's abdomen. His T-shirt was as soft as Yanmei's pink sweatsuit. Yanmei's ribbon fluttered on her wrist.

The girls were gone.

Nikki gritted her teeth to stop her eyes from tearing. Johnny had contacts all over the place, she reminded herself. He'd figure out where the Sun Yee On had taken Mingxia and Yanmei. Maybe Inspector Lam would be willing to bend a rule for one of Master Wong's charges, and go after the bastards who'd kidnapped the children.

Johnny slipstreamed past a line of double-decker buses as they emerged from beneath the harbor and into downtown. Nikki chanced a look behind and saw a single motorcyclist, with rider, pull around a colorfully painted tram. She wanted to ask Johnny if it was the Sun Yee On tail he expected, but didn't want to disrupt his concentration. The wind from oncoming buses buffeted the bike. Johnny held it steady and Nikki let out the breath she was holding.

They kept riding, well past the area where Johnny's tiny flat was located. The concrete, steel and glass buildings, relentless and towering, quickly gave way to shorter structures, and then they'd slipped out of the city into the cool, green lushness of countryside. On the bike, the temperature drop registered in chill bumps and a slight dampness on the skin.

Nikki thrust her face into the wind and inhaled.

Johnny's anger over the girls' loss was gone. Swept away by the crisp grass and dark earth, or simply faded from his mind and heart? All she could smell now was the woods surrounding them, and an occasional flash of oil and metal. And there— Johnny's own scent.

She shivered and hunkered closer to his warm back. One of his hands came off the handlebars to clasp lightly over hers where it lay on his waist. His belt ground into her hip bone. She ignored the discomfort. Being close to a warm, strong human being—to Johnny—was worth it.

The bike chased after the few yards of road its headlamp illuminated. That's what this mission to find Diviner had felt like from the start, Nikki thought. Only able to see *this* far in front of her and no more, with no hope of seeing anything more while a half-moon, satisfied with itself, cast a pale light over her shoulder. She wanted to see the end of the road, to read the book's last page, to fast-forward to the credits.

But she was going to have to get used to waiting for the road to unfold. They'd get there, wherever they were going, with that single headlamp. Diviner's container was on a slow boat to Singapore, and in a couple of days, she and Johnny would meet him at the port, take him into custody and contact Delphi.

And when Diviner was off their hands, she'd go after Mingxia and Yanmei.

She took a deep breath, this time to hold back a sob, and pressed her cheek into Johnny's solid, comforting back.

They rode up, over darkly green hills, and then Johnny had to use both hands to guide the bike along a twisting ribbon of single-lane road. Nikki leaned with him on the tight turns. She spotted the glittering sea passing in and out of sight as the road wound up and around the hills that separated downtown from the destination Johnny sought.

Then they were slipping down the other side of the range, and ahead the lights of a small town gleamed against the water that surrounded it.

Johnny slowed the bike, then abruptly switched off the headlamp. He turned the Ducati into the woods and Nikki realized he was following a narrow walking path away from the road. Then he killed the engine and, turning, put his finger to his lips.

Nikki remained silent, only twisted so she could see the road. Johnny had brought them several yards into a dense forest, and in the dark she couldn't see the road at all. Then light shuddered through the black and a motorcycle sped past.

When she started to move, Johnny shook his head.

A second motorcycle hummed by, then yet another high-whine sport bike. Three? The Sun Yee On had put three men on them?

Johnny motioned her off the bike. She quickly dismounted, as did he, and then he pushed the Ducati a little farther down the walking path. He turned the bike around to face the road and leaned it against a boulder. When he removed his helmet, she followed suit.

"Now we walk," he said, and his voice sounded muffled and lost amid the stubby trees and hardy scrub.

He took her hand and they trekked silently along the dirt path. Nikki felt a fleeting fear—nice place to kill a woman because they'd never find the body— but it passed the moment the forest gave way to a stony outcropping.

Wind whistled up the long, steep slope. Beyond the cliff's lip, the sea glistened, and Nikki could barely hear waves hushing themselves on the beach far below. Along a narrow spit of land, buildings outlined by their lights gleamed in the dark.

"It's Stanley Village," Johnny said. "Where the beautiful people live."

His faintly disgusted tone made her smile despite herself. "Why did you want to come here?"

"It's peaceful."

She accepted that because it was true. The ever-present traffic noise was muffled by the trees and hills, and drowned out by the wind. Nikki closed her eyes. Here, she could easily do what Master Wong had wanted her to do in his dojo: be present. Thoughts that had cascaded through her mind back at the terminal—Where are the girls being taken? Who are the Sun Yee On fighting now? Is the fight about Diviner or just a turf war?—faded, leaving her mind and heart open to simply being, to listening.

She became aware of Johnny's pain and loss spiraling around his body. The breeze shifted the fine hairs on her forearm. If she listened, she could hear small rustlings in the underbrush, as if chipmunks skittered.

"My father lived down there."

Nikki's eyes opened, but what she saw in her mind were the stripes and scars on Johnny's back. The ones she'd leaned her cheek against minutes before.

"He was an ambitious man," Johnny continued. "He hated waste and bad decisions. He told me often that he made a mistake marrying my mother when she got pregnant."

"Pregnant with you."

"Come, sit down."

He gestured to a squarish boulder set back from the cliff's edge. Nikki levered herself onto a roughly level spot. Johnny leaned back against the rock next to her. His face, profiled against the town's lights, seemed chiseled from the cliff.

"When my father was about twelve, he went to work for the Fourteen-K, a triad based at that time out of Shenzhen, just north of Hong Kong."

"What did he do for them?"

"Courier work, mostly, though he used to brag to me about being involved in human smuggling."

Nikki instantly saw the dying Cuban girl, skin parched, her neck and chest crushed from being packed into the shrimper's hold. "He did that as a boy?"

"Only until he moved into bigger and better

things. By the time I was born, he was working in a foreign exchange service downtown."

"Money laundering?"

"Partly. The business was as legitimate as a few bribed inspectors could make it. He climbed the corporate ladder quickly, which meant he had a great deal of influence in the underworld. Money and power were all he thought of." Johnny was quiet for a moment, then added, "We shamed him, so he never told his employers about us."

"Because your mother was a civilian? Not involved in a triad?"

Johnny shook his head. "It's complicated."

"You can explain it to me."

"Look, the point is that my father wished he didn't have a family. Sometimes such a wish is strong enough to be heard by the universe."

He shoved his hands into his jeans pockets, shoulders hunched as if against the wind swirling up against his back. "The Fourteen-K didn't know about his family, but the Wo Shing Wo did. My father was very good at his job. When he took control of a heroin shipping route the Wo had been trying to secure, the Wo sent an assassin after his family."

Nikki closed her eyes. The lights, so far away, were beginning to hurt.

"My mother was a good fighter. She had to be to live with my father. But the Wo killed her." He paused. "They didn't know they were doing my father a favor."

"What did you do?"

Johnny's head fell back to lean against the rock. His throat seemed somehow both strong and vulnerable. "I was thirteen. Old enough to kill a man."

Nikki was suddenly awash, drowning, in parchment and tattered leather binding. Beneath the regret lay a dim shadow of pennies, as if the years between then and now had helped him accept what had happened to him, but not his own actions.

She wanted to touch his shoulder, to put her arms around him, but sensed that to do so was wrong. It would be trying to fix something that could never be fixed. What comfort could he take from her? Why would she think he would respond to anything she might give?

"I'm sorry that happened to you," she managed to say, and felt her own tears slip over her cheeks.

"It's an old story." He shoved away from the boulder where she sat. "You told me about your gift. It seemed fair to tell you about this."

"Fat lot of good my nose did us tonight."

"The circumstances were—"

"It shouldn't have mattered."

"You did what could be done. You didn't fail."

"The girls were *right there!*" Nikki clenched her teeth against the pain creeping into her throat. "I should have been able to tell they were there."

"You should cut yourself some slack."

"Why?"

Johnny's hands lay heavy on her shoulders. "Because it does no good." He shook her gently, his face close to hers. "Because whatever you think is wrong with you doesn't define you."

Nikki leaned her forehead against his and inhaled. Pine from the trees. His skin. Brine from the sea. She was tired. Physically, mentally. Tired of not being able to know him the way she knew other people, by the signposts of their scents.

"I can't tell what you're feeling," she said in a small voice.

"Not ever?"

"A few things here and there. Regret when you talk about Regina Woo."

Johnny raised his head so they no longer touched. "What does that smell like?"

"Like being in a library full of old books."

He nodded slowly, as if considering what connection regret might have with moldy books.

Nikki could think of several: lost knowledge, the follies of humanity recorded long ago, forgotten love stories.

Had he loved Regina? Her chest tightened. "What happened to her? You gave me the abridged version, but you didn't tell me everything."

"I don't wish to speak of it."

"She was Athena. She was my sister."

"You never knew her."

"In my world, at Athena, we're all sisters."

Johnny was silent for a long, long moment.

"Were you lovers?"

"No."

"Then just say it. Tell me what happened."

Johnny's fingers tightened on her shoulders until she thought her collarbone would break. "It's ugly."

"Try me."

Anger tinged his voice. "I killed her."

Chapter 15

Nikki bolted off the boulder, heart thudding, and put some distance between them on the narrow ledge. Wind whipped up from far below, swirling her loosened ponytail. "How did you do it?"

Johnny stepped toward her. "It was simple."

She instinctively reached for the missing SW-99. "Gun? Knife? What?"

He stopped his advance and laughed, a sound dragged through deep sand. "Neglect. Stupidity. Carelessness." He paused. "Arrogance."

Rotting fish, Nikki recognized instantly. Self-derision. Self-hate. Johnny hadn't killed Regina directly. He'd made a mistake of some kind. She relaxed a fraction.

The rock beneath her foot gave, her weight shifted. She gasped as the ledge crumbled.

Suddenly she was crushed to Johnny's chest. Her feet lost contact with the ground. She spun, caught in his arms. Her wrist jammed between the boulder and Johnny's back. She yelped.

"You okay?"

His hand running through her wind-tangled hair felt nice. So did her legs entwined with his, and his pelvis pinning her to the rock. But other parts of her didn't. She grunted. "My arm."

"Damn. I'm sorry."

He released her. She wasn't quite out of reach before Johnny was running his broad hands over her forearm.

"Did I hurt you?"

"You scared the shit out of me." Nikki mentally cursed her unsteady voice.

"I shouldn't have said what I did. Not like that."

"Damn right, you shouldn't have. I thought I was your next victim."

His hands stilled. "I wouldn't hurt you."

"That's not what I was hearing." Nikki pulled her arm from his grasp. "You make me feel sorry about what happened to you and then tell me you killed Regina Woo? That's bullshit of the worst kind, Johnny."

"You're right."

"Then stop being coy and tell me what you're talking about. How did she die?"

He thrust his hands in his jeans pockets. Clouds were sailing swiftly overhead. The moon, what there was of it, disappeared. With the light gone, only the winking sparks of Stanley Village pricked the darkness beneath them.

"We were to meet after she left her work. I usually show up a few minutes early on days we start a mission. As a precaution. With my work, the men I associate with—it's good to be careful. To protect the mission."

Nikki resisted the urge to ask him questions about his missions, whatever they were. He'd paused again, and she didn't want to stop him.

After a moment, he said, "I was being followed. I saw her leave the office building and start walking down the street. Sun Yee On, I thought. I recognized the man following me. I lost him a couple of streets over, but by the time I got back to Regina…"

"You weren't the target," Nikki said softly.

"No, I wasn't."

She stepped close to him and breathed deeply. This time, she didn't need to see his face. He was telling the truth.

"She was a good woman," Johnny said. "Good strategist. What's the phrase? Grace under fire?"

"She was Athena. She *would* be good."

"Yes, I see that." He pulled his hands from his pockets and stared at them, not looking at her. "You both honor this Athena Academy."

"And you think you killed her."

"I should have recognized the decoy."

Part of her thought, *Yes, you should have.*

Another part of her said, "What does your grandfather say about it?"

Johnny took two long steps that put him at the cliff's edge. Nikki's knees went weak with sympathy. Would he jump? Finally he said, "My grandfather says I live too much in the past."

"You're not doing that now, are you? You're here, right now, with me. You're telling me about the past, but you're here."

He pivoted then and nodded. "Yes. For now."

"Can you stay with me? At least until we get Diviner?" When he didn't say anything, she added, "I need you to help me."

"I don't see how."

Nikki swallowed. "Everything's…overwhelming. I can't keep it all straight—"

"You're smart, you've—"

"That's not what I'm talking about." Tears threatened and she cleared her throat. "In me. It's overwhelming. Everything I feel. It's too much."

"You are…passionate."

"Out of control."

"No. Just passionate."

"You balance me." She paused because the next thing was going to be hard to say. *Give me strength,* she prayed, then said, "I can't do this on my own. You're the only one who can help me."

The clouds moved on, and Johnny was silhouetted, a black figure against a less black sky. In the silence, Nikki could hear cars purring along the ribbon that separated Stanley Village, refuge of the wealthy few, from downtown. She and Johnny seemed to have all the time in the world. This moment when they were both *here, now,* could stretch on forever and she was, for the first time in her life, content to let it do that even as part of her ached to have his arms pull her in, where she'd be safe.

"Yes, I will help you." Johnny drew close. "I'm sorry. About all of it."

"Me, too."

They stood together, barely touching. Nikki felt the same spark, the same awareness, that she had earlier in the evening. Still, the only scent she knew was the clean salt from the sea wind.

"You really can't tell how I feel," he said.

"No. Not right now."

He took her hand. She thought he was contemplating it, as if turning something over in his mind. Then he guided her palm to his chest.

Below the armor of hard muscle and unyielding bone, his heart thundered, fast and sure.

"Now you do."

Her mouth went dry and she remembered that kiss in the club, how he'd lingered and how she'd wished for more. And sometimes, she reflected as he bent his head and grazed her lips with his, the universe grants the wish it hears.

His hair was softer than she'd guessed, but his arm sliding around her waist was as solid as she remembered. He took his time. She'd been kissed before, plenty of times, but Johnny made her past boyfriends feel like *boys,* when he was so definitely a *man.* That feeling unnerved her.

As if he sensed her hesitancy, he eased off her lips and with his thumb tipped her head slightly to the side, baring her neck. His firm lips nibbled down her jaw to the sensitive skin beneath her ear. She gasped, inhaled deeply, and fell headfirst into a sea of the sandalwood scent that flared from them both.

Then he was back, angling his mouth over hers. She slipped into the *now,* feeling his breath on her cheek, tasting his lips and tongue. Her hands burrowed beneath his T-shirt and he groaned when her fingernails raked his back.

"Nikki," he growled.

A single step, and he pinned her against the boulder, his arm cushioning her head. The rock pressed painfully into her spine but she didn't care. His hot skin was all she wanted under her fingertips, under her body. When he tilted against her, she knew exactly how he felt.

The high whine of a sport bike razored the stillness.

Johnny abruptly released her. The wind cooled her heated face and neck, and she almost shivered.

"We have to go," he said.

He grabbed her hand and they ran for his Ducati, crashing through low branches and path-encroaching underbrush. The whine was still some way off.

"Should we wait it out?" Nikki asked.

"No. It's the first bike. They've doubled back."

The whine dropped an octave.

"They're looking for us now."

Nikki swung behind him on the Ducati's seat. She jammed her helmet on and held his ready for him. Johnny ignored it to key the bike running. He drove quickly, bouncing over ruts. Nikki felt the back tire fishtail, then they'd popped out of the forest and he'd turned them onto the narrow road, headed north toward downtown.

He gunned the bike up and over the summit. Nikki prayed the bike wouldn't leave the ground and one-armed his waist tighter. They curved and swayed quickly—too quickly, she thought—back and forth until they hit a straight stretch. Johnny reached back, snagged the helmet she held and levered it onto his head without losing speed.

Behind them, a crack broke past the sound of roaring engine.

They can't be shooting, Nikki told herself. She caught Johnny's faint penny scent and corrected herself. They *were* shooting.

"Hang on to me!" Johnny shouted.

Nikki didn't protest this order. She simply wrapped both arms around his waist and hoped their pursuer's aim at moving targets was bad.

The pursuing bike's whine dropped into more of a rumble.

"They're closer!" she shouted into his neck.

He guided the bike into the right lane—the oncoming traffic lane—and back to the left. Evasive

maneuvers. Nikki clutched his waist. Her back itched
and its muscles spasmed, anticipating a bullet's
stinging heat. Another crack, and a round sang past
her helmet.

"Get ready!"

What? To get shot?

On the other hand, would getting shot when you
were doing about a hundred and fifty miles an hour
away from the bullet mean you'd survive? Wind stung
her eyes and she forced them to stay open. She looked
behind. The bike's headlight glare masked the driver.
Then movement. A glint of metal shoulder-high.

"He's going to shoot again!" she yelled over the
wind and engine.

"Sit back!"

Johnny's body tensed. Nikki jammed her feet onto
the pegs and leaned hard. The Ducati's scream had
topped out. Now it abruptly dropped and Nikki
slammed forward, into Johnny's back, as he braked.
She rode up his back about a foot, clutched his shoulders to keep from being thrown over his head.

The other bike swerved, shot past them. One
driver, one rider holding a gun. Neither wore a
helmet. The rider's aim went wild. Johnny gunned
the Ducati. Nikki dropped back into the saddle. In
moments, she'd yanked off her heavy helmet and
held it by the strap.

"Alongside!" she yelled.

Johnny shifted gears. The driver was twisting his
neck, trying to find them. The rider yelled and

waved his gun, trying to get a clear shot. Johnny feinted passing on their right, then switched left and sprinted even.

Nikki leaned far toward the other bike and gave it her best home-run swing.

Her helmet thudded against the rider's naked head. Her arm bounced back. The armed rider swayed crazily. His driver slowed.

The bike careened in the middle of the road. Johnny sped up a hair to get clear. Nikki caught a glimpse of the armed rider falling. The driver shouted something and tires screeched on pavement.

Johnny shifted gears again and they pulled away. His victory whoop reverberated through his back, where she'd pressed her cheek. She couldn't get her breath, she realized when she started seeing stars. No breath, no shouting.

Nikki patted Johnny's chest with the hand still grabbing his rib cage. He nodded and began to slow, much more gently this time. She kept a grim hold on her helmet. She didn't look to see if the guy's brains were splattered on its shiny surface.

They hit the outskirts of downtown in minutes, and Johnny started his evasive maneuvers through narrow side streets that he'd done on the way to his grandfather's place the night before. The low-slung buildings that lay like foothills to the mountainous skyscrapers reeked of ginger, jammed grease traps and yesterday's fish. Nikki didn't dare hold her breath. She kept seeing the rider falling sideways, imagined him tumbling along the pavement while the motorcyclist slammed to a stop.

Johnny pulled into an alleyway and finally parked near some garbage cans. Nikki's hands wouldn't stop shaking. She was trying to breathe deeply, into the very bottom of her lungs. The stars had receded a bit, but the rotted fruit and meat brought bile into her throat.

And damn, her hand stung.

Then it was all too much—the noxious smells, the garbage, the rider falling into the road, the sound of the helmet smashing into his head. Nikki leaned on the wooden fence lining the alleyway. Her stomach, caught between wanting to retch and trying not to heave, clenched.

She felt Johnny's hand, strong and gentle, on her nape, then his other hand braced her forehead.

"It's all right," he murmured. "Be sick if you need to."

Great, just what she needed. A guy who ordered her around, was a chauvinistic pig one minute and a gentle lover the next, and who was about to do for her what not even her best friend had ever done. Not that Nikki would have asked… Erping up your guts was sort of a private thing.

But here he was, unfazed. It was enough to make a girl forget the chauvinistic pig part.

Nikki swallowed hard. "I'm okay. It's the odors."

"I didn't think about that. I'm sorry."

"Sensory overload."

"That ride didn't help."

"No, it didn't."

When she straightened, he stepped back, gave her room. She was sure her face was green in the sickly light cast from the seafood stall he'd parked behind.

"Are you okay?" he asked.

"Couldn't get my breath for a while."

"Adrenaline rush."

"The rush won't do me much good if I pass out."

"Here." He guided her back to the bike. "Just sit for a minute."

She hiked her butt back onto the bike's seat. "Do you know who those guys were?"

He shook his head as he laid a comforting hand on her knee. "Nor why they want to kill us now instead of follow us. Unless the Wo Deputy Mountain Master got pissed off by your bluff about the boat last night."

"Just what I need."

"It will be okay." He squeezed her leg.

The bad light slanting across the broad planes of his face made him look dangerous rather than ill. The pine surrounding him told her he'd either rubbed up against some sap on the mountainside, or that he was feeling particularly protective. Her face flamed when she noticed his untucked shirt. She'd done that. With a man she barely knew.

Except that she did know him. Quite a bit of him, in fact. Enough to know that if she was going to be caught in a mess with two Chinese gangs, miscellaneous evil women and in a country she didn't know squat about, this was the guy for her.

She caught herself up. No, the way she'd just characterized him was wrong, dishonest. Sure, it was true in its way, but not the way she meant. When he stood beside her, she felt centered. When he held her close, she felt safe. It was like her body knew in a way her traitorous brain didn't that he was good and trustworthy. His knowing his way around and being able to fight the good fight was just icing on the cake.

"There's another possible reason they were following us," he said.

Nikki thought for a moment, then her stomach warmed with dread. "They already know where Diviner's going. They don't need us anymore."

"It's the most logical explanation."

She stared at him. Nothing resembling fear emanated from him at all. "These jerks are out to kill us and we just nearly got killed at about a hundred miles an hour and neither of those two things bothers you?"

Johnny smiled. "It means we know what to expect in Singapore."

Chapter 16

The flight to Singapore was full up, and Nikki found herself breathing through her mouth. Johnny sat next to her, aisle seat, and said little during takeoff, for which she was grateful. She watched the low, lush mountains fall away as the plane gained altitude.

It was rare for her to have this kind of trouble with the scents these days. When the "gift" originally developed, back when she was thirteen and going through puberty, she'd had migraines from overload—horrible, gagging, sick-to-the-stomach migraines where everything physical, especially scents, was offensive. It'd been months before she'd learned how to filter out the unnecessary, before she'd discovered how to tell the difference between physical and emotional scent.

If her tracking of Mingxia and Yanmei was anything to judge by, she was still having trouble with that.

Johnny might be right. Her gift might be unpredictable.

She'd never tried to quantify its accuracy in any way—never thought that little exercise was necessary—but he had a point, she thought as she watched clouds slip like gauze across the window glass. How could they count on her extrasensory sense of smell if it went whacko on her or put her down for the count every other day? Heaven knew she had plenty of stress already in her life right now, and topping her days off with a migraine was an event she couldn't afford.

Four hours later, they landed at Changi Airport as a light mist began to fall. Johnny negotiated a rental car at the busy terminal, and by the time they had tossed their shared backpack in the Peugeot's trunk, the mist had strengthened into rain.

"Where do we get weapons?"

Johnny pulled out of the rental car lot and joined heavy traffic flowing toward an oasis of skyscrapers. "I have an old friend from the Organized Crime and Triad Bureau. He'll set us up with what we need."

He quickly left the highway and maneuvered the car through crowded side streets, dodging crazy drivers and crazier rickshaw cycles, until they reached a ramshackle part of the city. Nikki lost count of the number of times he doubled back, crossed train tracks and crept down alleyways. She couldn't tell if they were being followed, and she wasn't sure it mattered anymore.

Whoever had been hunting them down in the wee hours might, as Johnny suspected, already know Diviner's next destination and simply wanted to reduce the competition for Diviner's wares—whatever they were. And in that case, who needed to follow them?

"Are you just being careful?" she asked.

"After Regina?"

She shut up and concentrated on studying the leaning houses amid once-lush surroundings made thin by overdevelopment and made gray by the thunderstorm. People hurried everywhere, dodging puddles and carrying baskets of wares through the streets. At a crossroads, when the view opened up, she glimpsed the steel towers of downtown, architecture inspired partly by the East, partly by the West.

Johnny saw her looking and said, "My contact is in an outlying village. It will be safer there for us."

Nikki clamped one hand on the Peugeot's door handle as he swerved to avoid a car drifting toward them. Diviner's container was due to arrive late the next day, around seven in the evening. Another evening and day to kill.

Another evening and day to spend with someone she couldn't read unless he chose it.

Emote, dammit, she thought to him, and then blushed faintly because when he emoted, he *really* emoted. She ignored the low ache prompted by her too-damned-good memory.

He finally pulled the Peugeot into an alley that crept beside a well-kept house about a block long. As he set the emergency brake, he said, "Lee Wan is our host. He will give us food and weapons and a car. Stick with me, and don't smile at anyone."

She must have looked baffled because Johnny caught her chin in his hand. "Like the Electric Dragon. Only this time you *are* with me."

When she'd recovered her breath from his thoroughly possessive kiss, she stepped out of the car. The alley was the house's drive, she realized, and it was jammed with cars. She sidestepped a puddle and tried to get her brain out of the lust-haze Johnny had left it in.

A tall, skinny man with a hundred years' worth of laugh lines and clearly dyed black hair ducked out of a low doorway to meet them. He nodded and bowed toward Johnny, ignoring Nikki completely. To her surprise, he greeted Johnny in English.

"My friend! How long it has been!"

"Not long enough."

The skinny man's smile revealed perfectly white, straight teeth. "Come in. Family is here, but you are welcome."

Johnny shot her a warning glance.

So the family meant trouble. No smiling. Smiling at strangers had got her in trouble at the Electric Dragon.

They shed their shoes in the foyer next to rows of other shoes, and followed their host into a large, square room dominated by a low table covered with bowls of breakfast pudding. At least a dozen people sitting on cushions laughed and talked while they scooped rice porridge from a common dish. They seemed friendly enough on the surface. And there were as many women, dressed in stylish Western slacks and shirts, as men. Nikki started to relax a little.

Johnny took her hand and led her to the seats Lee Wan indicated. It was only when Nikki was settled cross-legged on the cushion that she realized conversation had utterly stopped.

They were staring at her.

Nikki tamped down the urge to zip up her windbreaker to hide the little bit of cleavage exposed by her fitted top. Her natural inclination was to smile, to show she was friendly, but she didn't dare. Instead, she stared back, meeting each of their frankly curious, hostile and leering gazes in turn. One of the young men, ponytailed and sporting a knowing look that spelled trouble in any language, winked at her. Johnny appeared completely unconcerned but Nikki smelled the pine beginning to waft in her direction.

"You are welcome at my table, Johnny Zhao," Lee Wan said loudly. "You and your friend."

The patriarch's pronouncement seemed to kick the manners into gear, and each person nodded politely as Lee Wan spoke their names in introduction. Han Su, the ponytailed man, flashed a charming smile that suggested he wouldn't mind getting to know her a little better. Johnny scowled.

Introductions finished, Lee Wan sat next to Johnny and wrapped his long, wiry arm around Mei, a twentysomething with short, stylishly cut hair.

"You haven't come to see me in a long time." Lee looked past Johnny at Nikki, and gave her an up-and-down inspection. "Where's Bai?"

Nikki felt her face flame. Johnny's jaw clenched and he steamed furious copper before he answered. "Bai's been history for a long time."

"She was prettier," Lee said bluntly. "This one is…"

"Feisty," Johnny finished.

Lee burst out laughing. Everyone at the table stared briefly, but this time Nikki had no desire to smile. At anyone. Johnny included. Han Su's gaze definitely gained interest. The young woman on his left tugged at his elbow, but he pointedly ignored her.

Johnny's near-ribald comment must have raised her in Lee's estimation, however, because he leaned around Johnny to say, "You are American?"

"Yes."

Lee gave Johnny a stern look. "Your trial, not mine." He whispered in his young woman's ear. She rose gracefully from her cushion to hurry into the next room. "How is your honored grandfather?"

"In good health."

"And his girls?"

"The Sun Yee On raided the dojo yesterday looking for us. They stole two of the girls."

Lee tsked and shook his head. "Lower than dogs, the Sun. But you and your grandfather are well?"

"Master Wong is a survivor."

"Your friend is unharmed, and for that I am glad." Lee bowed politely toward Nikki.

Johnny's lips twitched. "She pinned a Red Pole's hand to the floor with a *sai*."

Lee Wan's cackle sliced through the murmured table conversation, which faltered into quiet. "Whose?"

"Chen Hsien."

A stunned silence filled the room, then copper speared Nikki's mind with such force she sprang to her feet and backed off a step. Bowls scattered and broke as Han Su came over the table at her, a knife in one hand. She sidestepped the jab, avoided the sweeping arc as the blade sought her rib cage. Then she had his wrist in both hands and twisted in, toward his body, to take him facedown to the floor. His elbow stretched, straight and vulnerable.

"Drop the knife or I break your arm."

She was aware of Johnny standing between her and the rest of the men, knew that Lee Wan was there as well. Shouts echoed around the large room. Han Su, wiry and strong, tried to yank his arm away. She could barely hold him, so she stuck her toes against his groin and pressed in. His face went red.

"Fuck you, *gwai-poh*," he shouted, and for the second time, Nikki heard the utter contempt in a man's voice when he used the term. He didn't let go of the knife.

"Your choice."

She popped a palm heel into his elbow. The joint snapped like a strong, dry branch. His grunt escalated into a cry. The blade slipped from his stunned and useless fingers. A woman screamed. Nikki kicked the knife skittering across the wooden floor.

Then Johnny was yanking Han Su to his feet by the ponytail. The man clutched his forearm to his stomach, sputtered what she knew were obscenities about her. Nikki stood on the balls of her feet, hands in loose fists, poised and ready for another attack. The swirling array of emotion in the room threatened to overwhelm her senses, but she fought the effect.

Don't take it in, she ordered herself. It wasn't as bad as the opium. Nowhere close.

Lee Wan's voice knifed through the sudden quiet. "Where is your honor?" He got in Han Su's red face, wagging an admonishing finger. "Whose house is this? Who is your father's brother?"

Han Su opened his mouth, but Lee snapped, "Shut up. You have dishonored your father with your behavior. Take your wife and get out. You are no longer welcome here."

The young man, still holding his forearm, shot Nikki a murderous look. He made as if to say something, but Johnny took a single step forward. That seemed to be enough to change Han Su's mind, and he just jerked his head at the woman who'd clung to his arm during the meal. No one spoke as they left.

When the door slammed hard, Nikki found herself shaking.

Johnny's hands found her shoulders and turned her to him. "Are you okay?"

She nodded. "Thanks for the help."

He smiled at her sarcasm. "I knew you could handle him." He lowered his voice to say in her ear, "Feisty." A wealth of respect—and heat—lay in the word, then he said politely, "Come, sit down again."

Lee Wan bowed deeply toward Nikki. "My greatest apologies for my nephew's behavior." He frowned at his remaining guests, who now vaguely resembled a still-life oil painting. "I hope no others of my brother's family will dishonor my house as Han Su has done."

With great solemnity, a young man stood and stalked into the foyer, his wife following. Then another. And again and again, until only Lee Wan and his twentysomething were left with Johnny and Nikki in the suddenly overlarge room.

"I wondered when it would happen," Lee Wan said, but his voice sounded more tired than upset. "Misplaced loyalties. I tell you, Johnny, when the triads become stronger than families, they have become too strong."

Johnny said nothing, and Nikki guessed he was thinking of his own father choosing a triad over his wife and son.

"They cannot change the fact their only uncle was

a police officer, but they also cannot control themselves. How are we to live?" Lee Wan shook his head as if shaking off the regret that surrounded him, and turned to Mei. "Come, daughter, bring fresh tea for our guests."

"I thought your family worked for the Fourteen-K," Johnny said as he watched Mei clear away the broken tea service and bowls of food.

"Three years ago, just after I left the Bureau, they switched allegiance to the Sun Yee On."

Tears pricked Nikki's eyes. "So your family would have known where the Sun are taking Mingxia and Yanmei," she said in a low voice.

"The market's strong in Turkey, Australia and Kestonia right now. Sometimes the Sun boats come through Singapore. There is no guarantee."

"That'd be too much to hope for," Nikki murmured.

"We'll keep our eyes open." Johnny squeezed her hand beneath the table.

When Lee frowned in puzzlement, Johnny explained. "We're here on other business, but if there's a chance we can intercept the Sun smuggling boat, we want to retrieve my grandfather's charges."

"Of course. And this is why you need the car and weapons?"

"Among other reasons," Johnny said smoothly as he released her fingers.

"Come on, Johnny. What are you up to?" Lee Wan's sparkling black eyes settled on Nikki. "Or what has your feisty woman done?"

"Nothing serious."

"Don't be humble, boy."

Johnny grinned and winked at Nikki before he said, "The Sun and the Wo Shing Wo would be happy to see us again. We've pissed them both off."

"That's the Johnny Zhao I know!" Lee Wan clapped his hands in delight.

"What have you heard about the Spider Woman?" Nikki asked Lee Wan.

The older man's laughing face abruptly sobered. He turned to Johnny to say, "You never do anything by halves, do you, my friend?"

The two men studied the tea Mei was pouring. Unwilling to talk? Nikki wondered, or just unwilling to talk in front of her?

Screw that. "Do you know who the Spider Woman is?" Nikki asked.

Lee Wan stirred himself from his thoughts and shook his head. "No, no one does. She is only a name who has a long arm and powerful hand."

"What's she into?" Johnny pulled a bowl of spiced noodles toward himself and started lobbing spoonfuls on Nikki's plate. "Guns? Industrial espionage?"

"Rumors fly, my friend."

"But no one knows exactly what she does?"

Lee Wan shook his head. "Only that she's an…influencer, getting people to do what she wants."

"What does she want?" Nikki asked.

The old man shrugged his thin shoulders. "What all tyrants want. Money. Power."

Genetically modified women like me.

"Whatever drives her," Nikki said aloud, "if she's hired the Sun Yee On to go after Diviner, she's after whatever *he* has."

"If we can get to him before anyone else does," Johnny said around a bite of pork bun.

"The Wo Shing Wo ought to know where he's headed," she pointed out. "They're the ones who brought him into the country to begin with."

"If they do know, they're going to keep quiet about it. He paid them in vengeance for his passage."

"But they have to know by now that the Sun Yee On want Diviner, too." Nikki lowered her voice to say, "We're about to walk into another gang war. Hell, we don't even know which side was shooting at us last night."

Nikki had the uncomfortable impression that their exploits were gaining stature in Lee Wan's estimation. To get back on track, she asked, "What does this guy have besides information that makes him so valuable?"

"His information was already used to kill off the Sun Yee On second-in-command," Johnny pointed out. "Imagine information like that used on a large scale."

Nikki, who'd never really conceived of "knowledge as power" in that way, thought for a moment. "Blackmail."

"Yes. Blackmail, murder, price-fixing. Among other things."

Lee Wan nodded. "And by 'large scale,' you're talking about government agencies."

"Or governments themselves."

And building an army of superwomen might just help Arachne keep that power.

"That'd be a trick and a half," Nikki observed.

Mei, who'd sat quietly throughout the conversation, now carefully placed her teacup on the table and said, "But doable. The Chinese government struggles with the fine line between using the triads to keep order and keeping them under control."

"What control?" Lee Wan snorted. "They do as they wish, including raid the home of a well-respected man." He nodded toward Johnny, but Nikki guessed his deference was for Master Wong.

Johnny's jaw clenched briefly. "And kidnapping orphans."

Nikki wanted to curse the Sun Yee On, but the effort seemed pointless. Getting angry all over again wouldn't help her keep her focus. She'd learned that the hard way—when she'd forgotten her gift and lost the girls in the first place because she'd been so intent on being pissed off.

She had to do things differently this time.

"But with both triads after us now," Johnny was saying when she pulled herself out of her thoughts, "we have to be even more careful."

"You're here, so you've been suspended again. Making trouble?"

"It wasn't me," Johnny protested. "Nikki's fault entirely."

Lee Wan's eyes nearly disappeared in his laugh

lines as he regarded Nikki anew. "After what I saw today, I don't doubt you."

Then Lee Wan shook his head sorrowfully. "My stupid nephew, dishonored in his uncle's house."

Nikki felt a brief swell of sadness for Lee Wan until he added, "Bested by a woman! The shame!"

Chapter 17

Nikki woke, groggy, from a nap. The cinnamon scent that greeted her was real—physical—and was coming from burning incense. Not deep affection for a loved one. She opened her eyes.

Mei's sleeping room was about six feet by six feet, and held nothing but the narrow pallet Nikki lay on and a small table where the incense stick smoked. A mirror hung on one wall, and a pop group's glittering poster hung on another.

After the relative splendor of the dining room, Nikki had expected a larger room than this for Lee Wan's only daughter, but then, she supposed, the sleeping area was for sleeping and who needed all that extra space when you were just going to be un-conscious, anyway?

She closed her eyes and tried to hear past the walls and closed door. No voices outside, no clatter-ing in the kitchen, nothing. What day was it? Had Lee Wan and his daughter gone to work?

Nikki rolled off the pallet. She checked the mirror. Her hair had pulled from its ponytail, so she fished the band from the coverlet she'd slept on and stuck it in her jeans pocket. A couple of finger-combs got the curls more or less presentable. That was the ad-vantage of curly hair—no matter how badly it needed a brush, she could normally get it to look decent without one. She straightened her top. Her jacket lay across the pallet's foot, but she left it there. With "the family" out of the picture, she felt relatively safe in Lee Wan's home.

And hungry.

She slid Mei's door open. Not even a ticking clock greeted her. Maybe she should find Johnny first before she raided the kitchen. It'd be pretty rude to just snack down on leftovers without asking permission.

Double doors at the end of the dining area opened onto an interior courtyard filled with trees. Its flag-stone path wound through explosions of colorful plants where butterflies fluttered. Nikki looked up at the open roof where the trees grew well past the roofline. How had she missed seeing their tops pro-truding from the roof when she and Johnny had driven up? The flagstones were still wet from the day's rain, so she stripped off her socks and padded along the path into the yard's center.

There she found Johnny, shirtless, on his hands and knees, weeding the garden. Sun slanted through the open roof, lifting the damp into a muggy heat. She paused to admire Johnny's wide, sweat-slicked back, how the old scars did nothing to detract from his masculine beauty. She blushed when she saw the faint red scratches down his lower back. Had she done that with her nails last night?

He sat up to chuck a handful of weeds into a bag. "Hello." His pleased smile called up so many emotions, she was flummoxed for a moment.

"Hi," she said lamely. Then, because she felt like an awkward teenager, she went straight to business. "Did you get guns and a car from Lee Wan?"

"Yes."

"So we're ready to go."

"We will be when the time comes, yes." Johnny wiped his mud-smeared hands on a towel. "We'll stay here tonight and most of tomorrow."

"Unless we go looking for the Sun Yee On boat."

"Nikki." He tossed the towel on a wooden bench and took her hands. "I know how you feel about Yanmei and Mingxia. But every time we go looking for them, you risk your life. Will your goddess be pleased?"

Which one? she thought. Athena might be unhappy, but Hecate—the wild-child goddess of childbirth— would be all in. And there were times when Hecate's take on things definitely held an advantage.

She pulled from his grasp. "You don't have to remind me of my duty. I know what it is."

"But you're negotiating with reality."

"How do you mean?" Nikki slumped onto the bench beside his towel. She stuck her legs straight out, then thought her posture might look sullen and drew them in again.

Johnny knelt in front of her, placed his hands on her knees. "You know what you need to do, but you're trying to see what you can get away with."

"I'm not being sly," she protested.

"No, you're not." He started to say something, then closed his mouth. "Look," he tried again, "I'm not trying to tell you what to do or who you are. I'm just saying that I've been you. I've gone into gang fights and shot my mouth off and been a…" He frowned, then came up with a word. "Hothead."

"Works for me," she said, trying not to get annoyed.

"Does it?" His raised brow was skeptical. "It doesn't really work for me."

"I'm not going to get suspended."

"But you may get killed."

"Everybody has to die sometime."

"Do you want to die doing your job or doing whatever the hell you want?"

"These girls' lives are more important to me than anything else—"

"And your goddess knows that. But she still told you to stick with your mission. She made that choice for you. It's your duty to honor it."

Nikki sat back, arms crossed. She swam through copper as if it were water and she a fish. A small fish in a very big pond.

Johnny dropped his hands from her knees. He scrubbed the back of his neck with his palm and stood. "If you want to go to the port tomorrow, I'll take you."

"Lee Wan told you when the Sun boat might land?"

Johnny didn't look at her as he said, "He called a friend who owed him a favor. The Sun have a couple of boats coming here tomorrow afternoon."

"Before Diviner is scheduled to show." She leaned forward to take his hand, heart in her throat. "We can get the girls *and* Diviner."

"Only if one of the Sun boats is actually carrying the girls."

"Will Lee Wan help us?"

"Now you want to bring my friend into it?"

"He's a cop—"

"He used to be. Not anymore." Johnny knelt again, gripped her fingers hard. "This is negotiating, too, Nikki. What happens if that Sun boat does have the girls but the Wo show up looking for us? Do you think they'll show mercy on the children?"

"We can get them to Lee Wan—"

"Who's an old man. Do you want to see him dead?"

"He handled his family pretty well."

"Because we're taught to respect our parents beyond anything." His jaw worked for a moment. "Sometimes to our detriment."

Nikki ran her fingers down a long scar striping his smooth shoulder. His mother would have left her loving father, Master Wong, and gone to live with her husband. Never complaining and living with the abuse, Nikki guessed, just as Johnny didn't run away despite the beatings.

Because it was his duty.

"You defied your father," she said. "He wanted you to join a triad, didn't he?"

"This isn't the same."

"The hell it's not. It's exactly the same."

"I didn't have a choice between two rights." His voice was diamond-hard. "I had a choice between what was right and what my father wanted. It was not a choice at all."

And at that, Nikki had the surreal impression of a door opening deep in her mind. It was as if she'd been looking at a picture of a carefree young woman, and then something inside her eyes shifted just enough that she could suddenly see the crone's face hidden in the shadows. Johnny had lived with the injustice of being born to a father who didn't want him, had refused to follow in his father's path and had accepted his father's rage and shame literally on his own shoulders.

No one would beat her if she chose what her heart demanded. But what she risked was something much greater, as Delphi had said. If she allowed herself to be moved from her purpose, her scattered loyalties—her scattered mind and motives—might prevent her from doing her duty not just to Athena but to all the women who'd been modified by Lab 33. The women who were just as innocent as Mingxia and Yanmei.

"You're right," she said slowly, resenting what she was saying but saying it anyway. "If I buy it before we get Diviner, I'll blow the mission. And maybe Athena Academy. Or worse." She took a deep breath and said softly, "But I don't want to let those girls suffer. It's not right."

"I know. We'll get them back. If not now, then later. I swear it."

Her tears splashed on Johnny's wrist. She leaned into his strength as he gathered her close. She supposed she ought to feel foolish and stupid, but curiously she didn't. She believed him when he said they'd get the girls back. He was a good man—his grandfather had said so, and she knew it from experience.

That comforting certainty settled in her heart as his arms settled around her shoulders. He'd made mistakes, sure, but she'd seen firsthand his concern for the girls, his outrage over their kidnapping. He'd never have shoved her into an air vent and risked his life keeping watch if he hadn't wanted those children safe, just like she did. He'd keep his word about getting them back.

And it felt too good to just cry and be held and know that for whatever reason, this incredibly exasperating man accepted her, if only for this moment.

When her tears had spent themselves, she lifted her head from his shoulder. "Sorry about the crying jag."

He bent and kissed the moisture from her cheek. "Don't be sorry. I understand." His fingers moved in her hair, as if testing the waters and liking them.

His lips brushed hers then, moving gently. She gave herself up to the kiss, and let the clenched fist that was her angry heart soften. *Loose fist,* she thought. *Let the energy flow.*

Johnny deepened the kiss and the longing inside her chest blossomed into need. She couldn't help the little whimper that escaped her at his tongue's probing—how good he tasted—or at his hand's advance up her thigh.

"Nikki," he murmured.

"Please." She grasped his hair to pull his head back and ran her lips over his neck. She wanted everything, and she wanted it now.

"Wait."

She propped her forehead against his, breathing hard. "What?"

"We have time."

"You don't want…me." She tried to make the words flat, nonjudgmental, but she couldn't stop the little sob at the end.

He guided her hand to his pants. She gripped his marvelously stony erection. "I do want you, feisty thing. Smell me."

She tucked her nose into the joint of his neck and shoulder, and inhaled.

Cinnamon. Cinnamon laced with sandalwood.

Shocked, she raised her head to stare at him. His

black eyes, placid and trusting, remained steady on her face.

"Do you know how I feel?" he asked.

She nodded, afraid to speak.

"Then we have time, don't we?"

He gathered her close and kissed her gently. She let herself revel in his embrace, almost high on his scent. She wanted his arms, his hands, his mouth, his shoulders, his back, his scars, his arrogance, his stubbornness, his protectiveness, his nerve, his gentleness. She wanted the whole package. She wanted it now, but maybe, just this once, she could wait for it.

The waiting was bound to make it even better.

And when he broke the kiss to smile at her, she smelled more cinnamon rising up between them, and recognized it was her scent for him, and his for her.

Chapter 18

Cranes arced over the inlet of Keppel Harbor like massive yellow teeth. From the Port of Singapore Authority's locked sixth-floor observation room, she could see ships lying at anchor, waiting their turn to be off-loaded. At midafternoon, the cranes' beaks swung containers through the air and, beneath their huge steel legs, men in hard hats drove pickup trucks from warehouse to container stack and back.

The PDA she held in front of her body, shielded from the observation room's security camera, registered dozens of signals.

"A network in every corner," she muttered. She tipped the screen in Johnny's direction and showed him the leaping lines of wireless signals. He stood at her side, seemingly gazing out at the impressive sprawl of machinery that made Keppel Container Terminal one of the busiest container ports in the world.

"No special signal?" he asked.

She knew he meant Diviner. "Not from here." She scrolled through the list of signals coming through. No odd blocks and squares of the satellite transponder.

"Ms. Gao will be back in a minute," he warned.

"We have plenty of time. She'll have to unlock the door first."

"Humor me."

Nikki snapped the lid on the PDA and tucked it in her borrowed purse. Masquerading as freelance industry journalists for *Cargo Systems Magazine* hadn't been her best idea for getting inside the terminal, but it'd worked. She'd been surprised her claim of needing the PDA for her "notes" seemed to appease Ms. Gao, the marketing manager. Maybe the technology was commonplace in Singapore.

Ms. Gao had been very thorough in providing them a general rundown of the security measures the Port of Singapore Authority had in place at their container terminals. And if the magazine wanted to do a four-page spread on their state-of-the-art command and control system, she was honored to provide any information as was allowed for public consumption.

The observation room's door gave a heavy thunk before it opened. The business skirt Nikki wore was a shade too small—Mei's biggest suit felt skintight to Nikki—and she surreptitiously pulled it down a hair as Ms. Gao, a neatly dressed middle-aged woman, entered.

"Thank you for waiting while I attended to a phone call. I regret the delay." She smiled. "May I do anything else for you?"

"Your security methods are very impressive," Johnny said. "I haven't seen such a thorough setup in all our travels. Have you?" he asked Nikki.

"Not at all."

"We hope it will be permissible to speak with the head of security you told us about, Mr. Ali bin Sulaiman," Johnny added smoothly. He smiled.

Ms. Gao's smile widened. "I will see."

"Thank you."

She left the observation room again. The door snicked and locked behind her.

"So when she smiles, she means 'no'?" Nikki asked in a low voice.

"You're catching on."

"It's like talking to a wall."

"At least it's a polite wall."

"True."

"And it's consistent."

Ms. Gao stepped in again. Nikki wondered who or what the marketing manager had had to consult and how she was going to turn them down without saying no.

But Ms. Gao surprised her by saying, "Mr. Ali is in his office now. May I take you to him?"

"Please, thank you," Johnny replied.

On the trek down the brightly lit hallway toward the elevator, Nikki pondered what Ms. Gao had told them about the port security: armed guards inspected warehouses and other buildings at random intervals, the cameras were monitored by a team of security personnel at the command and control center, lights illuminated every inch of the port. There was no chance they'd be able to get in and out the way they had in the nether regions of the Kwai Chung terminal.

An irritated feeling in her chest began to kick in. Nerves. How were they supposed to catch Diviner— and his gear—when the place was crawling with eyes, both human and electronic?

Nikki tried to ignore the antiseptic smell of the elevator and then the fresh-carpet tang when the doors opened on the foyer. Another walk down a long hallway, through yet another locked door, and they were in a tiny reception room containing a desk, a telephone, a plain white box that plugged into the wall and a stern-looking man. One door behind the desk led to a glass-enclosed room. Another had a card swipe reader.

"Mr. Ali has been with us for several years," Ms. Gao said as she handed them off to the scowling man. "He will be able to answer any questions you may have." She smiled. "Mr. Ali or his assistant will see you out."

The assistant punched a button under the desk's lip with no small amount of resentment. "Please wait." The door to a glass-enclosed room opened.

The antiseptic smell was even stronger in the small space. In the sterile environment, Nikki identified her own antifreeze-scented impatience. She wanted to talk to Johnny, tell him they needed to find a different place and time to snatch Diviner, but was wary of saying anything aloud, just as they'd been in the observation room. And she was tired of being escorted around and kept in locked rooms.

She wondered if Mr. Ali could be trusted, Lee Wan buddy or no. And why would Mr. Ali help strangers only on a recommendation by Lee Wan? Was this all part of the honor thing?

Nikki forgot her questions when she saw an incredibly handsome man built along the lines of a basketball player and dressed like a businessman pause outside their glass room. He barked something at the assistant. A buzz, and then he ducked to enter.

Nodding pleasantly to Nikki and Johnny, he closed the door. It latched with the finality Nikki had come to expect. He stuck the clipboard he held under his arm to bring both hands together before his chest and bow. *"Namaste."*

Nikki echoed his movement, feeling absurdly like they were about to spar. Given his size, she'd lose. Given his beautiful, almond-shaped eyes, she wasn't sure sparring would be the most productive use of his time with a woman.

"Please, sit down." The man gestured to the pristine white table made of some indestructible substance and the chairs that fronted it. "I am Ali bin

Sulaiman. I hear we may have a mutual friend." He smiled widely at Nikki.

Uh-oh, Nikki thought.

Johnny stiffened in his chair. "My honorable friend Lee Wan sends his regards."

"Indeed. It's been a while since I've seen him, Mister…" Ali studied Johnny's badge. "Tan. And Miss Nikki Jackson." He scribbled on the clipboard. "How is my old friend?"

"Very well. Ms. Gao told you why we are here?"

"Yes, she did. You have come to the right place." His smile, beamed Nikki's way, broadened.

Johnny shifted slightly in the hard plastic seat. His voice was tight as he said, "I'm glad to hear it. We just have a few questions to ask you about your security measures."

"Please." Mr. Ali spread hands as lithe as a pianist's.

"I imagine you get many shipments from Hong Kong," Johnny said.

"Quite a few, yes."

"And special containers, with special requirements, are handled carefully?"

"Special requirements?"

"Out of the ordinary." Johnny took out his own little notepad and quickly sketched the four cat-claw strikes that would identify Diviner's container. "We have seen such containers marked as having precious cargo and assumed they need special treatment."

Mr. Ali regarded Johnny thoughtfully for a moment. "Please wait." Mr. Ali clicked a remote on his key ring. The door he'd entered arced open and he disappeared through it. Nikki heard a rapid-fire conversation between Mr. Ali's pleasant baritone and the aide's near-soprano, then nothing. In a few moments he returned and beamed a broad smile at them both.

"No, no special requirements at all." He settled into his chair again. "What else do you wish me to speak of?"

"We'd appreciate a look at the command center," Nikki said.

"I regret to say that today is not a good day to see the command and control center," Ali said. He glanced at the assistant outside, who seemed to be keeping a watchful eye on the interview in the glass room. "In fact, the Keppel Terminal is not the best place to see our security measures at all."

"Why is that?" Nikki asked.

"We have made many improvements to our security system at the Pasir Panjang facility." Ali angled his long body in the woefully short chair and flashed her a studied, polite smile. "It is by far the most secure area managed by the PSA." Then he sobered to say, "We are very fortunate in that the traffic is light at Pasir Panjang, as it is not yet completed."

"May I take notes?" Nikki asked, reaching into her purse.

"That is not preferable at this time." Ali's mobile face, dark eyes flashing, hinted at something she couldn't read.

Nikki withdrew her hand. "My apologies."

"No matter." Ali waved and his long fingers fluttered like a flirting woman's. "Security is security. I must beg your pardon as I make a note of my own about your visit. You are writing a magazine article?"

While Nikki recited their cover story, he wrote quickly on his clipboard with a felt-tip pen, in beautiful, elegant ideographs. Johnny made no move, appeared his normal stoic self, simply watched Ali's flowing strokes. She kept talking, rather inanely, she thought, about magazine layout, full-cover photographs, the article possibly turning into a cover story featuring a photo of Ali standing in front of the cranes lining the harbor. Ali simply nodded politely and kept scribbling.

"Thank you for the information," he said when she wound down. "I will see that a press photograph is sent to your offices immediately. To what address should I send it?"

Johnny gave him a Hong Kong address, which Ali faithfully copied down on his clipboard page. With a start, Nikki recognized it as the location of the Electric Dragon. Ali nodded again, and the smile that graced his face met his gorgeous eyes this time.

"I wish you great luck in your endeavors," he said as he stood. "My assistant will escort you out."

That was it? Nikki thought. *The bastard didn't say a thing.*

Ali bowed low, held it for a moment, then took her

hand and brought it to his lips like a graceful courtier. "Thank you for seeing me."

Johnny stepped next to her. In his movement, Nikki detected the curdled milk of jealousy. "You have been a very great help with our work," Johnny said. "Thank you."

Ali clicked the remote on his key chain. The door unlocked itself and rocked open. The stern young man stood up behind his empty desk. As she passed into the tiny reception area, Nikki caught a glimpse of Ali raising a brow at the young man—a clear look of "idiots, this Chinese and American," if she'd ever seen one—and then he slipped the paper from his clipboard into the white box behind the reception desk.

A grinding echoed in the room as the shredder chewed its way through the notes.

Johnny frowned at Ali's tall back disappearing behind a closing secure door. "He ignored us! Wasted our time."

"Don't worry about it," Nikki said. "Look, we won't put his picture on the cover."

The assistant cracked a smile, but whether it was of satisfaction or of the politeness masking his real thoughts, Nikki couldn't tell. "Please come with me."

Checking out was less tedious than checking in: dropping off visitor badges, signing the register, displaying again the fake IDs Lee Wan had given them, answering a couple of standard questions about whether they'd been left alone while on the premises.

Nikki opted for the truth on that question, and received a peremptory nod from the armed guard, as if she'd made a good choice about fessing up to being left for ten minutes in the locked observation room while Ms. Gao answered a phone call or peed or whatever.

Nikki slid into the Marindo sedan Lee Wan had loaned them for this little scouting trip and immediately kicked off Mei's heels. The girl had big feet, thank heavens, but that didn't make walking in three-inchers any easier. Nikki's toes and knees ached. She stretched out her feet and wondered why the whole chat with gorgeous Ali seemed…off.

Johnny slipped into the driver's seat, then made eye contact with her over a pair of rakish sunglasses that made him look like a hot actor from an action flick.

"Mr. Ali has quite a talent."

"Avoiding telling us anything?" Nikki retorted. "Lying through his teeth? Pretending to be Lee Wan's friend?"

"Writing upside down."

Nikki sat up straight. "You're kidding me."

"No, I'm not."

"What did he write?"

Johnny fished through Nikki's purse for a piece of paper and pen. "It was this."

He wrote the characters in English: TOSU 3099217 23:20. His intent gaze almost distracted her, but the numbers clicked immediately.

"The container code!" she said. "TOSU and those first seven numbers are Diviner's container code."

"The last four must be time of arrival. Eleven-twenty tonight. But you saw that place." Johnny cranked the engine. "We can't just walk in and grab the guy." He lowered the windows and a briny breeze cooled the sweat on Nikki's neck.

"No, but— Ali wasn't quite…right. There was something going on with him."

Johnny looked at her. "I know. The Singapore authorities are always uptight about security."

"Besides this," she said, waving at the paper.

"Yes, I know. Could you smell him?"

"Not really."

He turned to face forward and shot the sedan in gear, though he kept a foot on the brake. "Why not?"

"He wasn't emoting. Like you don't most of the time."

Johnny shrugged. Nikki got the impression the shrug was supposed to be casual, but it wasn't. "Okay, so what was going on?" he asked.

"Why is the Singapore government so careful?"

"Infiltration by triads. They've dismantled a couple of terrorist networks over the past few years, too."

"What? By playing Big Brother?"

Johnny frowned at the George Orwell reference. "What?"

"The government's watching them," Nikki clarified. "The cameras and the creepy assistant. All that."

"The port authority falls under government jurisdiction, yes, so Ali is accustomed to being watched."

Nikki played the conversation back in her head, word for word, gesture for gesture. "If he was doing the Ms. Gao thing, and every time he smiled he was lying, he was telling us that the security at Pasir Panjang isn't anywhere near as good as the security here at Keppel."

"You think he meant that's where this container is coming in?"

"He got serious when he said the vessel traffic was light there. Imagine the construction gear coming in and out. We'd have plenty of cover there."

Johnny nodded with the confidence of the half-convinced. He leaned his head back against the seat rest and sighed, then turned to look at her. "Then we'll need a plan when we go there tonight, won't we?"

"I think that's a very good idea."

Chapter 19

Nikki hunkered down next to a pile of rebar at the edge of the Pasir Panjang terminal premises. Here, the darkness was only sporadically pierced by light poles spaced far apart, and the one nearest her strobed off and on every few minutes. About two hundred yards south, under a glare of pure white light, a crane levered a container from a Hong Kong vessel. The crane's twin sat still.

She raised the field glasses and read the number of the container in motion. Not the one they were looking for. Wrong number and no red cat's-claw marks. Overhead, thunderheads piled up on each other. Nikki stretched out one leg, then the other.

She really wanted some barbecue: pork, ribs,

shredded beef. Shredded beef on a bun with a side of coleslaw. Or maybe *pollo con quimbobo y platanos,* chicken with okra and plantains, made the way her mother made it, with extra garlic and brown rice.

Johnny's black form solidified out of the dark, moving like a lean tiger. He knelt next to her, and she caught her breath at the scent that had become so familiar to her. The ninja garb he wore masked his identity but not his fiercely masculine form, and she deliberately turned her mind away from that line of thought.

"Any triads?" she asked.

"Not yet. The construction crews have shut down for the night."

"Good. How about the crane operators?"

"It's fly-by-wire," Johnny said. "They're in the main building, not out here." He pointed to the three-story building set well back from the cranes. "The unloading crew is still aboard the vessel."

Getting into the terminal had been a challenge, but nothing a pair of bolt cutters and a crowbar couldn't fix. She was holding out hope that Ali of the beautiful eyes had told his security team at this still-unfinished terminal to take the night off. There certainly didn't seem to be many badges out so far.

She checked the next container as it floated through the air. Nada.

"We may have guessed wrong," Johnny said.

Nikki tamped down her automatic annoyance.

"Yes, perhaps we guessed wrong. But if that's the case we won't be seeing any Wo or Sun bad boys, will we?" Overhead, a fizzing caught her attention. "You'd better get closer. The light's about to strobe."

Johnny slipped into the deep shadows with her. In about ten seconds the lamp overhead popped on, shuddered and died. "Nice timing," he murmured in her ear.

She didn't outwardly respond when his hand found her thigh; instead, she held the binocs to her face and tried to breathe evenly. "Are you over being jealous of Mr. Ali?"

"Almost." He dropped his hand. "The Wo second-in-command said Diviner paid to be put at the top. Shouldn't he have been unloaded by now?"

"Not necessarily. They're working their way bow to stern."

That meant another hour, at least, to wait. Nikki stifled a sigh. This mission had been nothing but one long wait after another. If she'd ever once thought she was patient, she'd been wrong. A crack of thunder, and a sudden rain shower, cold and driving, pelted her. Dammit.

The next container had just cleared the ship, arcing through the industrial-grade light cast down from the crane arms, when she smelled it.

Gasoline.

She touched Johnny's forearm to get his attention. "Someone's out there."

"Where?"

Nikki turned her head and sniffed past the metallic smell of a very real summer rain. "About a hundred yards east of here."

"Can you tell who?"

"No. But I think they're going to torch the place. They've got gasoline."

Johnny cursed. "Keep watching for Diviner. I'll be right back."

"Wait! The gasoline doesn't matter!" she stage-whispered, but he'd already faded into nothingness. Rain hissed on the concrete and metal, surrounding her in the cacophony of a snake pit.

Whoever was carrying the gas was going to run into a problem when they discovered there was nothing on the concrete docks and steel crane structures that would burn. The fire would simply eat up the gasoline and flare out without additional fuel. It'd be good for a diversionary tactic, but not much else.

She lifted the binoculars again, trying to angle the lens tipped down to keep them dry. When she got focused on the next container swaying precariously over the ship, her blood froze in her veins.

Four red streaks, like a cat's claw marks.

Diviner.

And no Johnny Zhao in sight.

Damn.

Well, there was The Plan, she reminded herself. If the Wo and Sun had had as much trouble as she and Johnny figuring out where the container was scheduled to land, she stood a good chance of being only one of two people who knew where Diviner was. Things might be going her way for a change.

Nikki smelled ozone, then lightning cracked, spewing a dozen fingers of light into the work yard. The lingering flashes showed men—about five— sprinting into the yard.

With a sinking sense The Plan was about to go down the toilet, Nikki abandoned her post. Weaving through shadowy, low-lying construction equipment got her within a hundred yards of the crane and close to the main building where the crane operators worked.

Focus on Diviner, she told herself as she wiped rain from her grease-painted face. Nothing mattered but tagging him and handing him over to Delphi. The triads were ancillary, a complication. She'd handle everything one challenge at a time, always keeping Diviner in her sights.

Nikki pulled the Russian pistol Lee Wan had given her from its shoulder holster. Water ran down the grip into her sleeve. *Gotta hang on to this one,* she thought as she leaned slowly from behind a front-end loader's massive tire.

Way too much rubber filtered into her nostrils, so that she couldn't smell the liters of gas the rabble-rousers had brought. That meant they could be anywh—

A hard hand clamped down on her shoulder.

Nikki popped her left elbow into the man's slick face. Cartilage crunched. He backed off, holding his nose, and she laid a front kick to his knee that put him on the ground. The pistol's butt took him the rest of the way.

She quickly turned him over. A young man with long, fashionably unkempt hair, he wore no distinguishing clothing, no marks or tattoos on his slender arms. Knowing her luck she'd just taken out gorgeous Ali's nephew. She rolled him up under the front-end loader's belly, out of the way and into the shadows.

One down and four to go? she wondered.

And where the hell was Johnny?

Voices warned her to duck under the loader's belly. She made herself small, drawn up into a nonhuman size and shape behind a rear tire. A few yards away, two pairs of drenched legs passed by in a hurry, spraying water with each step. The dark, muted clothing suggested triads, not security personnel whose shoes would have been in better condition and likely rainproof as well. She waited until they'd moved on, then exited her safe spot on the loader's opposite side.

High above her, swaying like a freakily shaped hanging fruit ready to drop, Diviner's container dangled. She flattened against the crane's massive leg, its cool steel chilling her spine. Here, at least, she was out of the worst of the rain. Could she take out these four, maybe five, guys on her own?

A dull thud impacted her eardrums. She spun and peered around the steel leg. The main building's top floor shot flames into the night, long strips of red and gold that would have been beautiful but for the plumes of black smoke and the stench of burning tar.

They'd found fuel, she gathered. Rain cast down like pellets before the fire.

She heard a startled shout and smelled the burnt coffee, then heard a grunt and silence. Then another cycle of shouts, coffee, grunt, silence. Music to her ears. It was Johnny.

Still, the container overhead hadn't moved.

Gunshots and shouts sounded behind her, near the main building. Car tires screamed. A chain-link fence slapped the pavement. Johnny was out there somewhere, and from the waves of copper that assailed her, everyone around him was pissed off.

Stick with Diviner, she ordered herself. *Stay focused.*

Ah, screw it. Diviner wasn't going anywhere. And Johnny might need her.

A bullet dinged the steel near her head. She ducked, looked for the shooter. A man armed with a handgun was running toward her, less than thirty feet away. He reached with his free hand to cock the double-action pistol; she dropped him with a thigh shot. Sprinting to him, she sweep-kicked the gun from his hand into the nearest block of shadow and followed it between two containers laid opposite the work yard from the ship.

"Nikki!" Johnny picked up the gun she'd kicked and tucked it into his waistband. "You okay?"

"Yeah. How many'd you get?" she asked as she

settled low next to him in the cramped space between the two containers.

"Three Wo soldiers, I think."

She swept the moisture from her face and rubbed her palm on her pants to dry it. "I got two…somethings." She kept watch over his shoulder, her stomach churning over the moaning of the man she'd injured.

"Those guys were Wo. The Sun just showed up."

"Great."

Johnny's hand roamed the modified bandolier he wore. "You still good for ammunition?"

"I'm okay. Used one bullet."

He nodded, and she smelled the clean rain of humor that enveloped him even in the real rain that surrounded her. "That's my girl. What's the smoke?"

"You missed the explosion? Somebody blew up the top floor of the building over there."

Johnny's head bowed. "That means they've killed the operators. Damn." His shoulders straightened, as if he were regrouping. "We've got about seven Sun in this area. I'll get them. You watch Diviner."

Then he'd leaped away and disappeared beyond the container stacks. She heard a thud, and the moaning man was silent. Breathing deeply, Nikki shook off her nerves. Better to get up top and see what was what.

The containers were too far apart to use her chimney-climbing trick, so she crept to the far end. Her luck was holding. One had an inset ladder, and she hustled to the container's top, where she lay flat. She rolled to the edge and looked down.

Men in black shuffled, dodged. Bursts of light sparked from their guns' muzzles as they fired. The tactical part of her brain thought she ought to have a rifle given her vantage point. The strategic part of her realized no one seemed to be trying to secure Diviner's container. Was that because it was trapped in midair? Literally hung out to dry?

The container she lay on shuddered beneath her. With a start, she realized great cables still attached to the metal framework had gone taut and were lifting, hoisting. A strong jolt on the scale of a minor earthquake, and the entire box rose.

Nikki skittered away from the edge as the container, now moving sideways, began to tip and sway. She got on her knees, stayed low for balance. Beneath her, shots spiked and bullets winged off metal. She turned to see where she was headed—

And froze.

The container she rode was aimed at Diviner's.

Damn.

Tucking the pistol in her shoulder holster as she went, Nikki scurried to the container's tether. Too thick to get her hands around and too slick with the rain to climb. She held on to the cable to look down at the concrete dock and the work yard that separated the ship from the container stacks. Too high to jump. The other side? She scrambled over. The ship snugged the dock and she didn't trust her spatial judgment to accurately drop her body in the tiny space between the ship's starboard side and the concrete into the harbor.

The crane arm that carried her stopped. Her container plunged toward Diviner's—she saw the rivets in the box he lived in—but didn't have the swing to make contact. Sickeningly, her container dropped back, drifting in its heady pendulum arc.

It jerked hard, throwing her to her knees. She clutched the rain-slick ridges and prayed her grip would hold. Maybe there was another way off?

Then she saw the man standing on the crane's arm, at roughly below her altitude. He stood on a small platform next to a guide wire attached to her container. The container, even empty, was too heavy for him to pull by hand, but he had hit the switch to start winding the container close.

He was gearing her up for another swing toward Diviner.

Nikki stripped her shoulder holster. She tucked the pistol in her waistband. Wind buffeted her back, but she managed to stay steady, on her feet. She looped the holster over the guide wire, grabbed it with both hands and jumped.

She fell fast, zipping down the wire. Rain blinded her, raked her face. Her booted feet aimed at the ledge the man stood on. A glint in the bright lights. A meat cleaver, gripped in his fist.

She couldn't let go of the holster to draw her gun. Still falling toward him, she drew back her legs, ready to kick away the knife. He reached up and hit something on the lighted control panel.

The bottom fell out. Her trajectory was suddenly

down, and she was almost free-falling. She clutched the holster tighter. The guide wire, slippery snake, plummeted with her. When it caught against its own anchor in the winch, it threw Nikki forward again, toward the crane's leg.

Nikki let go of the holster. She slammed into the lacey metal girder bracing the leg. Scrambled for a handhold. Slipped. Her fingers caught an edge. Panic clenched her muscles and she held, got her other hand up. The girder, slick beneath her grasp, was tilted, angled down at a diagonal. She hauled her lower body up. One ankle caught on the brace's top.

A gasp, a desperation sob. The ankle moved up and her knee hooked over. A final lurch and she had an elbow crooked. She pulled with that forearm, pushed with her other hand and scrambled up to straddle the beam.

She had to just hold on as tears coursed down her face. They fell, along with the rain, fifty feet to obliteration. Her lungs sucked hard on the oxygen her body couldn't seem to take in, seemed to want to thrust out. The sobs overtook her, wracking her body until her stomach hurt.

Nikki pressed her forehead to the beam. She had to get control. Shots still rang in the work yard below. Diviner's container still lingered, swaying slightly with the wind slanting the rain into her face. Her stomach protested, aching.

Jess wasn't going to believe this one.

Nikki shifted slightly. The pistol slipped free. She

watched it tumble over and over, shatter on the pavement below. A detached part of her brain gathered that she'd left the safety on. Or perhaps she hadn't racked another bullet into the chamber.

Whatever. It seemed silly now to think about it.

She cautiously worked her way backward down the brace she straddled. After a few minutes of creeping, her foot touched the crane's main leg. Thank God.

Nikki knew what she needed to do next: maneuver her butt against the metal leg and sit up to see her next step. She bit back a second round of sobs. Her arms, wrapped around the steel, couldn't let go. Not now. Maybe not ever.

I dare you, Rey's voice taunted her.

I double dog dare you, Frederico added.

She can do it, Jaime's voice said. *If she's not chicken.*

Nikki mentally shook herself. In the wide-open space between fear and need, she saw Jess's trusting eyes—*I believe in you*—and then, as if in an echo, Johnny's.

Diviner was her priority. Johnny was waiting for her. Assuming he still lived.

Nikki raised herself up enough to scoot backward on the beam. Her ass made contact with the crane's leg. She sat up.

Mentally giving her brothers the finger, Nikki took a deep breath and looked around for a means of escape. As she suspected, a rack of emergency handle-steps had been welded on the interior of the leg. Though they descended into a shadow and disappeared, she stood a good chance of getting most of the way down.

Now she only had to lean out about four feet to reach them.

Past the yellow girders that made up the cranes, Nikki saw Diviner's container move. Like a giant, unlikely spaceship, it ceased its hovering and began to descend swiftly.

She intended to meet it on the ground. Preferably armed. Preferably with Johnny and without any Sun and Wo soldiers who might be left.

Nikki gritted her teeth and swung her left leg over the girder, putting both feet on the same side. Equilibrium unbalanced, she tipped forward. Her legs tried to grip the girder but the movement threw her in the wrong direction. Desperate, she lunged for the rungs.

She caught them easily—were they not that far away? Heart thudding painfully, she paused to orient herself in a sane mental position—alive, not falling; panicked, but in a workable state. The rungs were narrow, but her feet gained surety as she headed down. And she'd nearly caught up with Diviner's container.

"Nikki!"

Johnny caught her in his arms as she plummeted down the last few rungs. He'd lost his head covering and the fear she read in his eyes, smelled on his skin, brought her repressed sobs to the surface. She clung to him, glad of his warmth and his hard arms around her, then pulled away.

"Diviner's—"

"We can't stay here," Johnny said. He gripped her hand and tugged. "The Sun have called in reinforcements."

Diviner's container crashed to the ground. Half a minute later, it rose again and waited twenty, maybe thirty feet off the ground.

Johnny ignored it and hauled her toward the container stack. "Here." He thrust a spare handgun toward her. "The Sun will be here soon. The triads took out each other, but I don't want to hang around for act two."

At the container stack, Nikki turned to study the container. Who was driving it? Why had it dropped and lifted again?

She instinctively sniffed. Sulfur? No. Phosphorous?

Nikki took a single step toward it, drawn to that cat scratch of a symbol.

The container exploded in a rolling fireball.

Chapter 20

Nikki found herself on her stomach, face ground into the pebbles and concrete, with Johnny on her back. Flaming debris rained down around them. She felt the sudden absence of his weight, then she was hauled to her feet.

She stumbled into the gap between two off-loaded containers and spun. Johnny had followed but fallen to his knees, reaching in vain for something behind him. Nikki shoved him around.

Blood gushed from a long slicing wound that stank. Burning flesh. She wrapped her hand in the untucked hem of her shirt. Tracing her fingers down the gash in his ninja garb, she found the shrapnel: a sliver of steaming metal the size of two fingers protruded from his left shoulder. She peeled back the torn fabric of his shirt. The sliver had come in from the top, at about a forty-five-degree angle.

In one swift movement, she plucked it out.

Johnny hissed but said nothing. Nikki dropped the sliver. Blood immediately welled in his skin's gap, about three inches worth of laceration.

"You'll need stitches."

"Later. It's not deep enough to bother with right now."

"Let me bandage it at least."

"No time. It's probably half-cauterized itself, anyway." He grunted as he straightened. "I saw a man running away from the container before it exploded."

"Diviner?"

"Probably. The two Sun soldiers chasing him think he is." Johnny turned, and his face was as impassive as if he'd never been injured. Just a little pale. "Let's get Diviner before the other Sun show up."

Nikki shoved her latest gun into her waistband at her lower back. "Which way did he head?"

"Toward the water. A boat maybe."

"Right down my alley."

"Good," Johnny said around a grunt. "I can't swim."

Nikki chose to ignore that and concentrated on creeping as quickly as possible toward the water. Johnny slipped ahead to lead the way. He hugged the shadows, both guns drawn and ready. In moments they'd crossed the wide, dangerous no-man's land of work yard and were back almost where they'd started, at the piles of construction materials awaiting the final phase of the terminal.

Johnny nodded toward a boatyard around the bend from the terminal. The chain-link fence didn't quite cut off the concrete bulkhead, and a nimble person could easily pivot around it without fear of falling into the harbor thirty feet below. On the other side, the lights of a sleepy-looking marina glowed a sulfurous yellow.

On the other side of the fence, Nikki sniffed. The wind had carried most of the scents away, but she definitely picked up the burnt coffee of fear. Diviner, perhaps, convinced he was running for his life from the gangs tracking him down.

You should have hung with me, pal, she thought, and clamped down on the mild hysteria that made her want to giggle because they had, after all, hung out together, after a fashion.

The coffee led her down a long slope of overgrown grass to the marina proper. She and Johnny knelt at the marina's edge for a moment, but no harbormaster or guard emerged from the office. The marina's five wooden piers stuck like fingers into this sheltered area of the harbor, the boats lined up in orderly rows.

In the distance, an engine—the distinctive engine of a cigarette boat—fired.

Two men sprang from a nearby boat and sprinted toward the far pier.

Wordlessly, Nikki and Johnny ran after them, Johnny quickly outpacing her. Nikki pulled her gun from her waistband and racked it as she ran. Amid the sailboat masts and fishing trawler gear, she saw the shutter-flicker of the men chasing down Diviner.

Johnny tackled the trailing man. They went down hard on the wood, scrambling.

Nikki sprinted past them and, as the leading Sun soldier tried to climb onto a private fishing boat, she bodychecked him. She caught herself on a dock line but the soldier teetered, then splashed. She wondered if she should go in after him, but he bobbed up some yards away and started swimming to shore.

"Good plan," she muttered to him.

Johnny joined her on the finger pier that ran alongside the fishing boat. "What now?"

Nikki climbed aboard the deep-sea fishing boat. "We go after Diviner."

Johnny shrugged as if to say, "Of course," and followed.

It took Johnny about fifteen seconds to break the lock on the main cabin door. Inside, Nikki hoisted the flooring. It slid smoothly up on hydraulic arms and an engine-room light popped on. A pair of powerful engines waited, gleaming with fresh paint and smelling faintly of diesel and antifreeze.

"Can you drive a boat?" she asked.

"No."

"Then start untying the lines. When you're done, go up on the flybridge. And hurry. This won't take long."

She dropped into the hatch between the engines. A bit of digging yielded a tool chest that had clearly never seen use. Nikki pawed through the wrenches until she found a long screwdriver with a rubber grip.

"Come on, baby," she coaxed.

She levered the screwdriver between the solenoid and the starter. The electrical connection made by her screwdriver kicked the starter into action. The abrupt rumble of the engine turning over jarred her hand, but she held the screwdriver in place until the engine was running. Mechanical clatter and roar filled the engine compartment.

Nikki quickly started the other engine, then hopped out of the hatch. Up on the flybridge, she checked the fuel gauge. Three-quarters full. She looked around to see that Johnny had released the last line and was safely in the cockpit, then reversed the big boat out into the channel.

Johnny climbed the flybridge ladder to join her. She flicked on nav lights and the searchlight, then gunned the boat well past the marina speed limit. If Diviner made the open ocean, he'd be lost to them for sure.

She veered around a marker and hit the main channel that led away from the terminal. She abruptly slowed the boat. Two directions, both lit up so brightly she couldn't tell if a boat was fleeing or not.

"You're about to learn to drive," she told Johnny. "Throttles here. Forward means go. Steer with the wheel."

"Can you smell him?"

"I'm going to try."

Nikki performed a fireman's slide down the fly-bridge ladder to the cockpit, then made her way along the narrow deck to the bowsprit. The constant wind was making this difficult. She gripped the rail and leaned forward, concentrated, let the scent that lingered on the air sift into her nostrils.

Brine and fish and old nets.

It was no use. Too many other factors were in play here. The wind had swept everything away.

The harbor's waves jostled the boat, which pitched and rolled without direction. Fitting, she thought. Deep waters, confused lights, thrown around by forces beyond her control.

No, that wasn't true. Her gift didn't belong to her for no reason. She hadn't spent the last eleven years learning to live with it—and use it—to back down now.

The South China Sea smelled different than the waters off Florida's coast. It rose and fell with the familiar rhythm of ocean. Water was ancient. Feminine.

Diviner wouldn't win this one. Nikki was in her element.

Master Wong's voice filled her mind, instructing her in her meditation: *Empty the mind. Hear every sound. Concentrate on it. Listen. Smell every smell. This is all there is. Open your eyes. See everything with a whole mind. Everything else—thought, word—is that which we create. It exists only in our minds.*

Nikki consciously relaxed. Her eyes opened

slightly, but she found it easier to keep them closed. Night herons barked. Crickets ratcheted along the shoreline. Waves slapped the boat's hull. She breathed deeply, consciously.

There, beneath the brine and fish and old nets, lay coffee. Stronger to her right than to her left.

She turned to Johnny. "This way! To the right!"

The fishing boat lurched forward. The turn came late, and Johnny overcompensated, but the scent remained pert, stringent in her nostrils. She waved at Johnny to speed up. The boat's engines kicked up a notch.

Still, despite the damp and the chill and the whiffs of diesel fumes when the wind blew strongly from behind, the fear-scent remained as if it'd been written indelibly on the air. Nikki sniffed at it eagerly until she realized her perception wasn't olfactory. It was something else entirely, something deeper and more fundamental than even this most primal of senses.

With growing confidence, Nikki directed Johnny to drive the fishing boat out of the harbor's mouth and into open sea. The sense of fear she recognized lay roughly south-southwest, speeding away, yes, but *there,* out past the roiling waters that churned at the junction of harbor and ocean.

She made her way back to the cockpit and climbed up the stainless steel ladder to the flybridge. Her sense of the fear was just as strong here as on the front of the boat.

"Where are we headed?" Johnny shouted over the engines as he relinquished the wheel.

"South-southwest, straight down the channel. Do you know this area at all?"

"No."

"There must be an island or something he's headed for."

A solid thunk struck the fiberglass near Nikki's knee. Johnny bent to investigate. When he rose again, he said, "Lucky shot."

"Are you a better shot?"

"On the water? All this motion?" He raised his hand up and down, mimicking the fishing boat. "Not a chance."

Still, he flicked off the navigation lights, plunging the instrument panel into darkness.

"Now let's see them hit us," he said.

Diviner shifted course to due south, Nikki noted, and changed her own course to match. He was starting to slow, apparently either reaching his destination or thinking he'd lost them. The shoreline to port had receded into the distance, and the channel markers disappeared. They'd hit open water.

Nikki swerved the fishing boat to port and slowed. "Let's see who's on our tail." The engines quieted and for a long moment the only sound was of their wake catching them up, hushing along the fiberglass.

A smaller speedboat, maybe a thirty-footer, sped past, slamming the three-foot seas unmercifully.

"Have a helmet ready?" Nikki asked, wishing she could see Johnny's face.

Then she knew, abruptly and without reservation, the humor was there. Without the scent.

"Got it right here."

Nikki heard the slide of a 9 mm being racked.

"You may not need one. They're beating their boat to death on the waves. It'll break soon."

He laughed at that. "Do we get that lucky?"

She thought about falling through space. "Sometimes. It's a gas-powered boat," she advised as she shoved the throttles forward.

Johnny grabbed the console to steady himself while the boat tipped her chin up and gained speed. "Am I aiming high or low?"

"Do you want to sink it or blow it up?"

"Sinking's fine."

"Aim just below the waterline. I hope they've got life jackets."

Johnny snorted.

In moments the fishing boat's powerful engines had brought them within yards of the smaller powerboat. Nikki flipped on the searchlight and beamed it straight at the passengers, temporarily blinding them. "Do it!" she shouted.

Johnny let a volley of rounds fly. Solid thumps sounded from the powerboat's hull. "That's it!"

Nikki flipped off the searchlight and dropped back. She heard Johnny loading a fresh cartridge in the 9 mm. "You want another pass?" She let the

fishing boat drift a bit to keep it from casting a silhouette against the distant lights.

"Do I need one?"

Nikki smiled. He was that confident in her abilities, or in his? She settled her mind, reached out—
and there was the abject terror of drowning.

"No, we don't," she said somberly. "Radio for the
Coast Guard or somebody."

Johnny plucked the VHF radio mic from its
holster and dialed up the hailing channel. Nikki
turned on the GPS to get a fix on the sinking boat.
After a few moments of conversation, Johnny
switched off the radio. "The Singapore Coastal Aux-
iliary is on its way."

"We'd better bail, then. Unless you want to hang
around and explain gunshots."

"That can wait until after we've brought Diviner
in."

Nikki's attention swung back to finding the man
she'd come halfway around the world to find. It was
a bit like splashing radar, she thought as she sought
the remnants of his fear. If something bounced back…
There. The fear bore a unique signature she was
learning to recognize as uniquely Diviner's. It *felt*
different than the fear of the triads in the sinking boat,
than her own terror as she dangled from the crane.

She withdrew the fishing boat to a safe distance
and waited until the flashing red lights of the rescue
team's cutter arrived. Johnny leaned against the console with her, watching. The searchlights the cutter

sported illuminated the men—four in all—pulled from the drowning boat.

"That's it for them," Nikki said. "Diviner next."

She was about to throttle up when she sensed Johnny's protective instincts kicking in, coupled with deep affection and something else she couldn't quite name. It was for her, all of it, a bouquet of emotion unadorned by ribbons or elaborate vases but clutched in a willing and eager hand. Not quite raw but not practiced, either. Pure cinnamon.

Moved, Nikki captured his face in her hands for a swift, hard kiss.

"For luck," she said gruffly.

"Do we still need it?" he asked, and she discovered she honestly couldn't say.

Chapter 21

Singapore, a country made up of a couple of dozen inhabited islands, had ample places for a clever man in a boat to hide.

Nikki knew where he was—it was getting to him through the maze of islands that was the problem. Especially in the wee hours of the morning with no moon to speak of.

Why couldn't she have stolen a boat with a working radar?

The GPS system aboard the fishing boat showed her three islands marching south, well off the main Singapore island. If she had to guess, her nose would say that Diviner was headed directly toward the middle island.

But why weren't these islands lit up like the

others? With as tight as the real estate was in this region, Nikki was surprised that three relatively decent-size islands hadn't been built up or on.

Ahead, the first island's outline warned her to slow. She throttled back a bit and checked the depth finder. She aimed the boat farther to the right, away from the sandy spit that might lurk off the island's western tip.

"Would you take the helm?"

Johnny moved into position. "What are we aiming for?"

"Due south on the compass. Maintain this speed. Keep an eye on the depth finder. The propellers will hit bottom first."

"Right."

Nikki pulled Delphi's cell phone from her pocket. "It'll be a minor miracle if this thing works."

"I saw the jump." Johnny's throat worked for a couple of seconds. "I bet the phone's trashed."

She found it safer not to reply. Her nerves stretched, taut and ragged, ready to let go in a moment of weakness she couldn't afford. Save the crying jag for later.

The cell's battery housing had cracked at some impact and separated from the phone. The battery itself looked okay, given what little Nikki could see in the steady dimness of the instrument panel. She slid the battery panel onto the phone's back. It snapped into place and the status bar lit up.

Bingo.

Nikki hit the speed dial for Delphi. In the distance, lights from a shipping vessel pricked the dark.

"Yes," the computer-altered voice said.

"We're almost on Diviner," Nikki reported as she scanned the darkness for an out-of-place light that might signal Diviner's boat. "What do you want me to do with him when we have him in custody?"

"A team is on its way. They'll meet you in the Strait of Malacca for the handoff." Delphi gave her lat-long coordinates for the rendezvous. "Will you need help getting out of Singapore?"

Nikki looked at the phone. Built-in GPS tracking? she wondered. She put it back to her ear. "Probably. We stole a boat and half the Pasir Panjang terminal blew up because Diviner had some kind of self-destruct sequence on his container."

"Are you okay?"

The darkness pressed in on her, deep and unfathomable. Nikki swallowed hard to keep her voice from shaking. "Yeah, we're fine."

"I need you to bring him in alive. And retrieve his electronic gear, anything that will help us find Arachne."

"Right."

"If Arachne gets her hands on Diviner…" Delphi didn't have to say more.

"She won't."

For a long moment Delphi said nothing, and Nikki thought perhaps the connection had faded. A breeze kicked up, bringing with it salt and cool water and the distant promise of more rain. Finally, Delphi said, "Good work."

"For Athena," Nikki said.

"For Athena."

Nikki shut the phone. "My boss has given us a rendezvous point in the Strait of Malacca. Assuming we can get to Diviner before the Sun Yee On shows up with reinforcements."

"We should be prepared." Johnny steered the boat a touch closer to the looming hulk of a pitch-black island off to starboard. "This guy might be meeting someone."

"Or he might just be running from the gangs trying to catch him," Nikki pointed out. "All evidence points to him being pursued by these two women, The Spider Woman and the giant who hired the Wo Shing Wo."

"But if the giant knew about Diviner, why didn't she just have them take him while he was aboard the Wo vessel?"

"Maybe she didn't know Diviner was valuable. She could have hired them after something came to light." Nikki studied the shoreline, how the jagged trees stabbed themselves into night-darkened sky. "I mean, some guy traveling around in a shipping container kitted out like an apartment might just be eccentric, not somebody important."

Johnny gripped the wheel with both hands as a rogue wave chopped at the fishing boat, shoving it sideways. "And these women discovered what made him valuable when…what? When he gave information to the Wo second-in-command about his enemy in exchange for a ride from Florida to Hong Kong?"

"That's what I'm thinking. If the Spider Woman is interested in information, it means she has a lot of contacts. She either knows people or can buy them. Maybe she wants more than that." Like Nikki herself, for mad scientist experiments in secluded and terrifying laboratories.

Nikki laid a hand on Johnny's forearm. "Wait. Throttle back."

"What is it?" He put the boat's engines in Neutral.

"I can see the tops of those trees."

"Village lights on the other side."

"We stopped seeing villages when we got out of the channel an hour ago." She reached out, scented the wind. It *was* Diviner, just on the other side of the island they were slowly approaching. "He's here."

"On land or water?"

She concentrated. "On land."

The faint glow behind the trees faded.

Nikki pressed the engine stop buttons mounted on the helm. The sudden quiet made her realize Diviner would certainly have heard their approach. A clearly resourceful man, he could have booby-trapped the island during the time it had taken her and Johnny to find him.

On the other hand, he hadn't expected to be

forcibly hatched from his container in the middle of a firefight, had he?

Maybe he was as in the dark, quite literally, as they were.

The fishing boat drifted closer to the island and the furry outlines of trees began to take on solid shape. Here, in the island's lee, the waves had smoothed to a gentle roll, and each shoulder shrug of water washed the fishing boat a few feet toward the shore. The only sounds were the slap of waves against the fiberglass hull and the shifting trees.

"Let's anchor and go ashore," Nikki whispered.

"I can't swim."

"It's okay. I'll drop the anchor off the bow and let the stern drift in. It'll only be about three feet deep."

Nikki slid down the flybridge ladder to the cockpit, then made her way to the bowsprit. The anchor was a manual job, so there was no noisy electric winch to broadcast their intentions. Johnny helped her release the heavy anchor from its housing and dropped it quietly into the water. Nikki measured the anchor rode with her arms as she lowered it, counted ten feet.

"Let's give it a minute to settle in," she whispered. "The wind will blow the stern closer to shore."

"Good."

"Come on."

Nikki led the way back to the cockpit. The boat rocked hard in the waves, canting over toward the shoreline. She slipped her holster off and lowered herself down the stern-mounted swim ladder. The cool seeped into her skin as she toed for the bottom. Just a few feet down, about chest-high for her. She still had to hold her gun and holster up over her head.

"It's not deep," she whispered.

It was odd, she thought as Johnny slipped into the water after her and they started to walk toward the island. No sound coming from the land at all. No crickets, no birds, no rustlings of small animals.

Nikki took two steps and dropped in over her head. She immediately kicked, to regain the surface, and kept her gun high.

"Wait," she whispered to Johnny, who'd stopped short. "There's a hole or something."

She frogged backward toward him, then used her booted toes to feel the hole's edges. A broad circle, easily ten feet wide, etched the sloping bottom. Nikki waved Johnny around to follow, which he did, with seemingly infinite patience. Nikki crept forward more slowly after that, slipping once and nearly going under, but managing to do a one-armed tread out of the hole.

What could possibly be making these craters? she wondered. The only thing she could think of was… *Shit.*

She grabbed Johnny's sleeve and pulled him close. "This is a firing range. The holes are from shell strikes. That's why there's no village. No lights."

Johnny exhaled a warm breath on her neck, then said, "We need that luck now."

"It's standard military ops to sweep the area

before the shooting starts. We weren't challenged, so maybe our luck is holding."

"Maybe. They might not have seen us."

"Any armed forces would've spotted us on radar. I think we're good."

They were soon slipping silently through waist-deep, then knee-deep water, grappling along the rocks protruding from the sandy bottom. Nikki cautiously raised her body from the lapping waves, hoping the incoming waves would mask her movement. Johnny caught her ankle. She looked down. He motioned to her right. She nodded. He'd go that way, she'd go the other. They'd put Diviner between them.

She knelt on the rocky beach to buckle up the holster and check her gun. The darkness was dense enough that the fishing boat, though so close, seemed more like a shadow than an object. She tuned out Diviner's nervousness enough to check her immediate, physical surroundings: old cordite, scrub trees and damp underbrush, a gathering thunderstorm to the south.

More phosphorous. What was Diviner getting ready to blow up now? Would he take himself out to avoid capture?

Nikki slinked into the lush, leafy underbrush, following the phosphorous scent. To her own ears, she sounded like a small herd of rhinos. Mosquitoes buzzed her face and neck. Every couple of steps, she paused to listen and sniff.

Rustling trees several yards away could be Diviner. Her nose said it wasn't. Maybe he'd set up some sort of diversion to send them off-track. She ignored the noise and continued more to her left, following the bitter coffee seeping through the leaves.

A boat's engines—gas and powerful from the rumble—roared in the distance. Nikki dropped to her knees and waited. The rumble gained volume. A spotlight swept over the water to pause on the beach, then aim up, in her direction.

Was it the Singapore armed forces who'd just discovered the trespassers' presence on the live firing range or was it Arachne's Sun Yee On soldiers out to kidnap Diviner? Or kidnap her?

No time to hang around, she thought. Johnny should have circled the small island by now and be on its south side. The boat approaching the island's north shore throttled down behind her. Its hull ground against rock and sand—the sound of the boat being beached, hard. Loud voices and splashes followed almost immediately.

The spotlight's beam cast her shadow toward the southern trees. Within seconds, bullets pitted and splintered the trees around her.

Forgoing silence, Nikki sprang from her hiding place and headed for Diviner's scent. She stumbled into a shallow shell crater filled with rank water, caught herself, scrambled up the other side. Behind her, men shouted at each other. The cascade of bullets tapered off. They'd apparently figured out they were more likely to kill their prey than capture it with their tactics.

She rounded a tree and paused to locate Diviner. His scent remained strong. He hadn't moved. Maybe she could flush him out and directly into Johnny's path.

She heard footsteps coming from the water, heavy-sounding steps that pulverized sticks and kicked aside rocks. Definitely not Johnny, and Diviner had appeared to be a skinny guy. This triad didn't think he needed to hide. And he smelled rank—of stale sweat.

Nikki stepped out from behind the tree to face his looming form silhouetted against the dim light cast from the boat's spotlight. He spotted her and started a lumbering sprint, then splashed headlong into the crater.

Don't think about it, she ordered herself. *Don't think about what you have to do.* She held the 9 mm steady, arms straight, her weight balanced. Maybe twenty yards away.

She let him clamber up to the crater's lip. He paused to catch his breath. She fired. The bullet struck home, low in his thigh. He yelped. Arms pinwheeling, he fell backward into the crater.

Too late, she smelled piercing, overconfident lemons. A fist caught her cheek. The blow spun her and she went down, right eye stinging. She turned the spin into a sweep, took the triad's feet from under him. His back had barely landed and angry copper spouted from his pores when she popped his solar plexus with the handgun's butt. Air whooshed from his lungs. He rolled away from her to get his breath. Still on her knees, she angled a swift strike at his neck's base, knocking him out.

Now, how many triads had been on that boat? she wondered as she levered herself to her feet. Plenty, from the pounding and crashing coming up from the beach.

"Nikki!"

Johnny's voice sounded desperate and several yards away, but she sensed nothing from him amid the rich humus and dead leaves of the island's groundcover and the salty sea. Heart pounding, she ignored the triads behind her. If Johnny had been wounded again... A few dozen steps forward brought her to the narrow island's southern shoreline that tipped delicately into the water. She reached out with her senses...

And was smothered in Diviner's coffee fear.

Instinct made her duck. A square, silver object whiffled over her head. She threw a waist-high back-kick, caught something soft, vulnerable. The man half grunted, half howled, and dropped the bludgeon onto the rocks. The clean rain of Johnny's humor wafted through the trees.

Gunfire—from two guns in the same area— exploded through the trees lining the shore. Beneath the cordite and Diviner's fear-sweat, she found Johnny's natural spice and the acrid smell of his burnt flesh. She glanced up to find the twin flashes marking the muzzles of Johnny's guns. The shouting triads crashed backward through the forest, apparently in retreat.

"Get him up!" Johnny urged.

While he provided cover, she grappled for the man she'd downed and who still lay groaning in the sand.

Diviner.

She knelt and gripped his thin shoulder. "If you want to live, you stick with us. Do you understand me?"

Diviner nodded weakly. In the pale light of false dawn, she could make out his razor-thin mustache and beard, black against his nearly white skin. His flesh hung flaccid on his frame, but he probably didn't care to spend much container living space on a treadmill. Such a peanut of a guy to be so much trouble and wanted by so many people.

Then Johnny stood over them both, guns held at ten and two o'clock. "How're we doing?"

"We gotta get back to the boat." Nikki gave Diviner a little shake. "Where's your gear? Did you blow it all up?"

He nodded.

"Except for that." Johnny jerked his head to Nikki's left.

The silver, mud-smeared laptop teetered on the rocks, inches from the lapping waves.

Shit. That's what he'd tried to hit her with? Nerves ratcheted long past overstretched, Nikki snatched up the lightweight computer. She crammed it under her arm and clamped on to Diviner's thick wrist with her free hand.

"Got a plan?" she asked Johnny.

He shrugged, keeping his eyes on the forest, where men scuttled and thrashed like beetles in straw. "How many did you subdue?"

"Two."

"Then we might get back to the fishing boat. I'll draw them to the east."

Johnny took off noisily before Nikki could protest, and the triads began crashing after him in the forest darkness. Almost immediately, shots shattered the air, but whether they came from Johnny's gun or a triad's, Nikki couldn't say.

She forgot her frustration about Johnny's abandonment when Diviner asked in a surprisingly deep and calm voice, "Where will you take me?"

Nikki breathed deep. He was still scared—the coffee bore that out—but the strong cilantro said he was also angling for something that he thought he'd get. Sly dog.

"You're going someplace where gangland heroes won't chop your bits off for fun," Nikki retorted.

"What do you want? Money? I can divert millions to an account for you."

"You're starting to sound desperate. Move." She jerked his arm and sent him stumbling in front of her along the shoreline. For good measure, she nosed her gun's muzzle against his kidney.

His hands shot into the air above his head.

"Not money? All right then. Information. What do you need to know about your enemies? I can ruin them in seconds."

"You've been hanging out with the wrong kind of people. I don't have personal enemies."

"What about this?" He waved a hand at the gunshots now cracking east of them.

"That's business. Keep walking."

He kept silent while they plodded through the wet sand and jungle fringe, and they soon arrived at the northern shore.

"There." She pointed with the gun at the fishing boat nodding peacefully at anchor. "Keep your hands on your head. Go. And forget about swimming away. I'm the least of three evils you're dealing with."

Diviner turned to regard her evenly before nodding.

Nikki followed him through the deepening water, guiding him around the holes. She kept the gun aimed at his back while he climbed into the cockpit. Cracks and an occasional shout broke the island's stillness. The impulse to abandon Diviner and go after Johnny itched her legs and prodded at her gut, but she managed to ignore it. Duty first.

When she mounted the swim ladder, Diviner sprang up the flybridge ladder. Nikki took her time getting into the cockpit while he scrambled around. She slid the fishing boat's salon door open and set the laptop on a seat inside, then closed up again.

"If you're looking for keys, there aren't any," she said. "Get your ass back down here."

Diviner did as he was told. In the brightening dawn light, he looked even worse: dark eyes sunk deep in his pale face, a rough five o'clock shadow bruised his sallow cheeks, his black hair limp and sweaty.

Moments later, Johnny lifted himself up and over the stern. "All clear," he said, as if he'd been weeding the garden. He eyed Diviner. "You should be tied up."

Diviner's eyes widened, as if Johnny had pronounced a punishment worse than death.

"I'll trade you anything you want to know if you cut me loose," he said. "It's what I do. Give me an hour, and I can give you anything."

Annoyed, Nikki almost said something bitchy, but stopped.

Mingxia. Yanmei.

This man, with his mind and his machine, might be able to give her the destination of the boat that had taken the girls away. Part of her claimed that was absurd—the triads didn't keep their trade routes in databases—but another part reminded her that the man in front of her, who was now trying to push glasses that weren't there anymore farther onto his nose, had delivered into the Electric Dragon's hands the life of his enemy.

He could deliver the lives of those children into her hands. Where they'd be safe.

"The Sun Yee On kidnapped two little girls—" She broke off.

Diviner nodded. "Yes. Their leader—what's he called?"

"The Dragon Head," she said automatically.

"The Dragon Head sends encrypted e-mails to his liaison officer at a bank in downtown Hong Kong. Schedules, payments, everything goes back and forth." He snorted. "Asymmetric algorithm encryption is *nothing.* And the network in the bank?" He made a scoffing noise, as if insulted. "Flypaper before a sword."

Nikki stared at him in the dawning light. Behind his head, the lights lining the far Malay shore gleamed a little less brightly and the water edged from black into dark grey. His skin, even paler now in contrast to his dark eyebrows and mustache, made him a gaunt ghost.

Diviner. He who detects truths. The discoverer of secrets. The discerning one.

And the minute he gave Nikki the information she wanted, he'd wipe his laptop clean of the information Delphi needed to trace Arachne.

Nikki let her frustration tighten into a clenched fist deep in her stomach. Feel it, she thought, and let it go. She waited, trying not to judge the feeling or herself, trying simply to accept the emotion as true at this moment. What could she do about the situation right now? Nothing. Not a thing.

After a few breaths, the frustration dissipated, leaving only her sense of what she must do and sadness that she must do it.

"No." The word was a gaunt ghost, too, wafting up like the old tome scent of regret, of anguish that things had to be this way, and no other. "Your offer's no good."

Johnny was looking at her, his eyes wide with understanding. He wasn't offering approval, she realized, but respect.

"Tie him up," Nikki said gruffly. "I want to finish this."

Chapter 22

"His name," Delphi's digitally altered voice said, "is Martin Slobojvic. He's a Kestonian national wanted in two dozen countries for computer piracy and industrial espionage."

Nikki stood alone in the center of Master Wong's sparring mat, holding the cell phone, now wrapped with tape, to her ear. The high-pitched giggles of little girls echoed in the kitchen, echoed through Nikki's heart. Yanmei's ribbon tugged at her wrist. She pulled herself back from the sadness to ask, "How long has he been living in that container? The man was fish-belly white."

"From what we've been able to determine, almost fifteen years."

Nikki whistled. "Long time not to see the sun."

"He kept on the move. The shipping records are spotty, but he's just been moving from port to port."

"Did you crack his laptop?"

"That and the disk drive your security friend, Ali bin Sulaiman, recovered from the container. Rigged to self-destruct if tampered with, as we expected, but not unbreakable."

"'Asymmetric algorithm encryption is *nothing*,'" Nikki murmured. "Did he have a right to be so arrogant?"

"Yes, he did. The laptop is the tip of the iceberg. He built a network of machines to hold pieces of data."

"Keeping everything spread out," Nikki mused.

"And out of the hands of his enemies. Arachne would have had a field day with the information he's uncovered."

Diviner of secrets.

But your secrets are being found out, Nikki thought. One by one.

"Will you be able to find Arachne now?"

Delphi seemed to wait, perhaps thoughtfully, perhaps pondering how much—or how little—to tell Nikki. "We have a better chance than we did."

"And the giant? Chang's descendant?" Nikki asked, referring to Arachne's possible rival.

"We're investigating."

And that was all Nikki anticipated getting from Delphi. She swallowed as the girls laughed again, and she heard Johnny teasing them. He was doing one of his story voices again.

"Are we done then?" she asked through a closing throat.

"Yes. Good work. You've done more than you know."

And less than she'd wanted.

"For my sisters at Athena," Nikki said as the tears fell, unrestrained and unjudged.

"For us all."

Delphi hung up.

Nikki stared at the phone for a full minute. She was enveloped in cinnamon, then in Johnny's arms. He buried his face in her loose, curly hair.

"We've been here for two days," he murmured. "You are rested?"

"Physically."

"Good. I've talked to Bai."

Nikki tensed. Johnny held her more tightly and chuckled. "She knows a few things. You should give her a chance."

"What *things?*" Nikki retorted. She angled out of his embrace and glared at him.

Still smiling, he rested his broad hands on her shoulders and squeezed. Grounding her, she realized. In the here and now.

"What did you talk about?" She sounded like she was strangling, but at least the words came out.

"Did I tell you she used to be a Sun Yee On liaison officer's lover?"

Nikki's eyes widened. "No. You left that little detail out."

"She says she talked to him last night, which means she was doing with him what you were doing with me."

Nikki's cheeks warmed, but before she could say anything, he added, "And he said something about the slaver ship making a fueling stop between Singapore and Kestonia."

Nikki forgot her embarrassment as adrenaline—liberally mixed with wild hope—surged through her. "When?"

"Tomorrow night. How long do you have left on your vacation?"

"About a week."

Johnny nodded. "That should be enough time."

Nikki grabbed his arm. "We can do this, yeah?" The waterworks were coming on strong again, but with him, here, it was okay.

"I have our plane tickets already."

He gathered her close and whispered, "After we return here, we should figure out why we're living on the other side of the world from each other."

She pressed her face into his chest and breathed deep. Here he was, all cinnamon affection and sandalwood attraction, his hard arms banding her back and his heart beating, strong and sure against her ear. Yes, they'd figure that out, and how they could change it.

Nikki pulled from his embrace but stayed close, her hand on his arm.

"Yes, we will. But first, let's go get our girls."

* * * * *

Turn the page for a sneak preview of the next
Athena Force adventure.
FLASHPOINT
by Connie Hall
Available April 2008

Puerto Isla

Lucy Karmon, still clutching the remote detonator, stared through the special fiber-optic scope at the burning meth lab below her. Pieces of the structure mushroomed into a spectacular cinder cloud, two hundred feet of it, masking the night sky.

On the ground, the rebels responsible for supplying Puerto Isla with everything from black tar heroin to Jamaican sinsemilla ran for their lives. Some men, their clothes aflame, dove into a stream at the bottom of a ravine.

Mesmerized, Lucy watched the symphony of destruction opening up before her. This is where she thrived, in the middle of uproar, mayhem, a world on the brink, a world she created and controlled. It touched a chord within her, an odd inner peace, a place that she desperately craved. Her mind settled into the calm and grew still. She observed the fallout, the wind shift, the added perk that she'd taken out the van and an old Pontiac Bonneville parked near the building. Mission accomplished. Target annihilated. But what could she have done better? Less fallout, perhaps. That equaled less C-4. Maybe she should have used Danubit or Demtex explosive. But she'd been correct in avoiding TNT. Too volatile and subject to the high humidity on the island.

She always questioned her work. Dissect, assess, moderate and estimate: DAME. She had perfected DAME at the Athena Academy for the Advancement of Women, a highly specialized college prep school for young women. Lucy could still hear Mrs. Warren, her junior year demolitions instructor, saying, "Strive for excellence. Anyone can destroy with explosives, but can you raze the target without loss of life? Can you tear down the ant hill without harming the ants? Refinement of the art, ladies, that is the key. DAME will help you not only in demolitions, but in any aspect of your life. Remember the old dame well, and she will always come through for you."

It had been her friend Val's glowing descriptions of the school in her letters that had intrigued Lucy.

She had harbored restlessness in her that she could hardly control. "Rebel Lucy," is what her mother had called her when her tutors complained about her lack of attention. Lucy just hadn't felt challenged. Monotony was her enemy. She had always found her father's work more than interesting, and she had invented her own engineering designs just to keep from dying of boredom.

By age eleven, she could design and place explosive charges to bring down either a whole structure or simply a wall within that structure. It hadn't seemed to impress her father, though.

In several letters, Val had suggested Lucy write to Christine Evans, the principal at the Athena academy, and apply. Lucy thought getting accepted into the academy might please her father, since nothing else ever had, so she took Val's advice.

She had described her fledgling engineering designs and the knowledge she had gained from her father. She had been a ninth grader at the time. Most students entered the Academy in the seventh grade like Val had, so Lucy figured getting into the school was a long shot. But to her surprise, she had received an acceptance letter.

She considered her years at the academy the most important of her life. It had taught her wilderness survival, martial arts, how to focus her physical and intellectual energies and discover what she excelled at: demolitions. Somewhere along the way Lucy learned to find self-worth and confidence, and to achieve new heights to please herself—not her father.

Now thoughts of seeing her father again made

her wish she were heading to Area 51, the Mojave
Desert, New Zealand, even the South Pole. Anywhere in the world but the same room with Roy
Karmon. There wasn't a room, a house, a castle or a
country big enough for both of them. Talk about py-
rotechnics. At least her mother would be there to run
interference and put out the blaze. Hopefully.

nocturne™

The Bloodrunners
trilogy continues with book #2.

The hunt meant more to Jeremy Burns than dominance—
it meant facing the woman he left behind. Once
Jillian Murphy had belonged to Jeremy, but now she was
the Spirit Walker to the Silvercrest wolves. It would take
more than the rights of nature for Jeremy to renew his
claim on her—and she would not go easily once he had.

LAST WOLF
HUNTING

by RHYANNON BYRD

Available in April wherever books are sold.

Be sure to watch out for the last book,
Last Wolf Watching, available in May.

SN61785

Silhouette®

Romantic
SUSPENSE

Sparked by Danger,
Fueled by Passion.

The Taken

Tierney Doyle is used to being criticized for
her psychic abilities, yet the tough-as-nails—
and drop-dead-gorgeous—detective has no doubt
about what she has uncovered in the case of a
string of unsolved murders. And Tierney is slowly
discovering that working so close to her partner,
detective Wade Callahan, could be lethal.

Look for

Danger Signals
by Kathleen Creighton

Available in April wherever books are sold.

REQUEST YOUR FREE BOOKS!

2 FREE NOVELS
PLUS 2
FREE GIFTS!

PASSION GUARANTEED SEDUCTION

YES! Please send me 2 FREE Harlequin Presents® novels and my 2 FREE gifts (gifts are worth about $10). After receiving them, if I don't wish to receive any more books, I can return the shipping statement marked "cancel". If I don't cancel, I will receive 6 brand-new novels every month and be billed just $4.05 per book in the U.S. or $4.74 per book in Canada, plus 25¢ shipping and handling per book and applicable taxes, if any*. That's a savings of close to 15% off the cover price! I understand that accepting the 2 free books and gifts places me under no obligation to buy anything. I can always return a shipment and cancel at any time. Even if I never buy another book, the two free books and gifts are mine to keep forever.   106 HDN ERRW 306 HDN ERRL

Name _____ (PLEASE PRINT) _____

Address _____ Apt. # _____

City _____ State/Prov. _____ Zip/Postal Code _____

Signature (if under 18, a parent or guardian must sign) _____

Mail to the **Harlequin Reader Service:**
IN U.S.A.: P.O. Box 1867, Buffalo, NY 14240-1867
IN CANADA: P.O. Box 609, Fort Erie, Ontario L2A 5X3

Not valid to current subscribers of Harlequin Presents books.

Want to try two free books from another line?
Call 1-800-873-8635 or visit www.morefreebooks.com.

* Terms and prices subject to change without notice. N.Y. residents add applicable sales tax. Canadian residents will be charged applicable provincial taxes and GST. This offer is limited to one order per household. All orders subject to approval. Credit or debit balances in a customer's account(s) may be offset by any other outstanding balance owed by or to the customer. Please allow 4 to 6 weeks for delivery. Offer available while quantities last.

Your Privacy: Harlequin Books is committed to protecting your privacy. Our Privacy Policy is available online at www.eHarlequin.com or upon request from the Reader Service. From time to time we make our lists of customers available to reputable third parties who may have a product or service of interest to you. If you would prefer we not share your name and address, please check here. ☐

SILHOUETTE

SPECIAL EDITION™

Introducing a brand-new miniseries

Men of Mercy Medical

Gabe Thorne moved to Las Vegas to open a
new branch of his booming construction
business—and escape from a recent tragedy.
But when his teenage sister showed up pregnant
on his doorstep, he really had his hands full.
Luckily, in turning to Dr. Rebecca Hamilton for
the medical care his sister needed, he found
a cure for himself....

Starting with

THE MILLIONAIRE AND THE M.D.

by *TERESA SOUTHWICK,*

available in April wherever books are sold.